honeycraves

I. S. Belle

Kindle eBook ASIN: B0D2WJ9VJH

IngramSpark Print ISBN: 978-1-067014-14-8

Amazon KDP Paperback ISBN: 979-8-332302-90-9

content warnings

Underage drinking, violence, murder, nonconsensual blood drinking, consensual blood drinking, beheading, discussion of suicide, addiction.

To the ones who always come back.

*"The woods are hungry, dark and deep.
Something, something, miles, sleep."*

—— *a misremembered poem from Sadie Greer
and Honey Williams*

chapter
one

SADIE GREER WAS HUNGRY.

A hunk of meatloaf sat in front of her on the cafeteria tray, untouched. Sadie hadn't eaten human food in a while. Not since her ex-best-friend-turned-girlfriend Honey Williams made her a vampire last year.

She bent over the meatloaf, inhaling the tacky, stale scent. It was disgusting, but it was easier than paying attention to the constant crush of bodies in the cafeteria, heartbeats thudding appetizingly under their flimsy skin.

Her stomach clenched. She ate a deer yesterday, but the hunger was back again. It still hadn't faded into something manageable, like Honey's had. It had quietened a *little*—a storm instead of a hurricane—but it was nothing like Honey's, which was a gusting breeze at worst.

The crowded cafeteria surged with life. Heartbeats pounded louder and louder, threatening to overtake Sadie's senses.

Sadie dug her fingers into the underside of the table, carving strips of plastic with her blunt nails. Then she looked over at Honey.

Honey was at her usual table, watching Summer demonstrate something with her makeup brush. Her lips were shiny with gloss, her strawberry blonde hair bouncing as she threw back her head in a laugh. Then the laugh stopped and Honey went unnaturally still. Her hand came up, fixing her bangs to hide the look she snuck over at Sadie's table.

It was so fast a human couldn't catch it. But Sadie saw it, clear as day: Honey's pink lips curved in a smile, shooting her a wink. Then she turned back, focusing on Summer's makeup brush.

Sadie extracted her nails from the underside of the table. It didn't make her any less hungry. But looking at Honey always brought her back to herself. She wished Honey could look at her from less of a distance, but they both agreed after the debacle at the start of the year that it was safer if they pretended they didn't hang out in public. Just in case another hunter came to town or some other YouTuber started making true crime videos about them.

Sadie watched Honey type something into her phone. A moment later, Sadie's own phone vibrated: *Playground l8r queen?*

Sadie snorted and texted back a middle finger emoji and a heart emoji.

Just a few more days, she told herself as she put her

phone back on the table. *Then spring break. Then a few more months of school. Then California, and the rest of our lives.*

Sometimes it comforted her. Other days it just reminded her how long their un-lives would be, and how much horror might await.

Two full thermoses of squirrel blood didn't do much to tide Sadie over. She texted Honey as she headed for the playground, so focused on a string of eyeroll emojis, trying not to focus on the raging hunger in her stomach, that she didn't notice the guy walking toward her until she barreled into him, knocking him onto the path.

He landed breathless on his back on the cracked concrete. For a second he just lay there, dazed.

"Ow," said Alexander White eventually with a pained laugh. "This is...not how I pictured it going."

Sadie stared down at him. It had been a long time since a human walked up to her without her noticing. She didn't think she'd been *that* distracted.

A vein pulsed hard in his neck. Sadie forced her gaze up to the guy's face.

"Help me up?" Alexander held out a calloused hand. It didn't suit the rest of him—everything about Alexander boasted of wealth and privilege. His perfectly coiffed blonde hair, his ironed polo shirt, his slacks and expensive sneakers. He was new to town, two years younger than her, and still acted like he was doing her a favor by talking to her.

Sadie stared at the prominent veins in Alexander's wrist before hauling him up.

"Whoa," he said as she effortlessly pulled him to his feet. He gave her tall, skinny frame a once-over. "You're stronger than you look."

Sadie didn't bother answering. She straightened her shirt—her worst flannel shirt, only worn on days she knew she was going hunting—and stalked past him toward the playground.

"Sadie!" Alexander jogged up next to her, smiling like butter didn't melt. "Got any plans for spring break?"

"No." Sadie walked faster towards the waiting playground, the swings waiting behind the slides. She could already smell Honey's peach body soap.

Before she could step over the wooden barrier onto the playground bark, Alexander shouldered in front of her. "Can't even give me a second? Hear me out, I promise I'm worth your while."

Sadie thought about shoving him aside. Instead, she pulled up a brittle smile. "Give me the spiel and get out of my way."

"I'll be fast." Alexander pocketed his hands, playing at bashfulness. It only made him look like more of an asshole. "They finally opened that new Italian place on Bleeker Street. Would you want to go with me? Maybe tomorrow night?"

"I'm not a big fan of Italian."

"That's fine! We could get coffee instead? Or go on a walk? You guys have some great parks."

Sadie stared at him, then at the sad park surrounding them. "Our parks suck."

"Maybe I just want to spend time with you." Alexander beamed like he was posing for a polo shirt catalog.

Sadie entertained a brief fantasy where she slammed him into the slide and sunk her fangs into his neck. Opening up the carotid artery. Drinking her fill, *finally*. She hadn't been full in so, so long.

A flash of movement caught her eye. Sadie looked behind Alexander and found Honey leaning against the slide in an exaggerated mockery of Alexander's stance, cheeks sucked in to imitate his wide cheekbones.

Sadie held in a snort.

"What?" Alexander started to turn.

Sadie grabbed his thick shirt. She waited for his cocky smile to falter, uncertainty shining through. Then she leaned in.

"Go bother someone else," she whispered, and strode past him.

In the time it took Sadie to intimidate Alexander into leaving, Honey had vanished. Sadie walked around the playground and sat down on a swing. The rubber was fraying, the chain covered in rust. This playground had been falling apart when they were kids. Now it was an outright health hazard.

She waited for Alexander's fast footsteps to fade.

Sure enough: *whoosh*. Honey leaned against the swing chain, her voice mockingly deep: "*Got any plans for spring break?*"

Sadie kicked at her. Honey dodged, sinking into the swing. For a moment Sadie's hunger faded into the background as she watched the soft curve of Honey's cheek in the afternoon light. Once they had been so small their legs couldn't touch the ground. Now here they were, tail end of senior year, still sitting next to each other on these creaky swings.

"Why here?" Sadie asked. They didn't usually risk the park. Not enough places to hide if someone walked past.

"Felt nostalgic." Honey toed a heart into the playground bark. Her smile sagged, making Sadie's nerves spark. Honey had been holding something back for the past few weeks. She kept insisting she wasn't hiding anything, but Sadie wasn't buying it.

As fast as it vanished, Honey's grin came back, blazing. "Also we have SUCH great parks, didn't you hear?"

Sadie groaned.

Honey cackled. "He was *so* lucky you didn't bite him. I *told* you he wants to sleep with you."

"He doesn't want to sleep with me," Sadie argued. "He's a true crime enthusiast. Or something. *You* said he was gay!"

"I said he has a gay mouth."

"That's not a thing."

"Maybe he has a *bisexual* mouth," Honey suggested, pouting in an imitation of Alexander's pillowy lips. Still pouting, she said, "Maybe he's one of the hunters Elijah warned us about."

Sadie snorted. They'd already dug into that—they couldn't find any evidence that Elijah and Alexander ever knew each other, let alone that they were part of the same freaky club hunting the vampire scourge of America.

Honey continued, "How's the hunger?"

"Awesome. Love it." Sadie picked at her hair. Any day she didn't eat, it grew limp and oily. Honey's strawberry blonde curls stayed shiny and springy until day three or even four of no blood. It didn't make sense—Honey only turned into a vampire a week before Sadie. They should be at similar stages.

She sighed, pushing herself up. Bark crunched under her feet. "Alright. Let's go terrorize the local deer population."

Honey didn't move. Sadie turned to find her leaning back in the swing, smiling knowingly.

"Actually," Honey said, "I have a surprise."

Sadie narrowed her eyes. It should've set off alarm bells in Sadie's head. She already knew what she should say: *It's too dangerous. You know how I get. We shouldn't.*

But she was so hungry. And it wasn't like they'd be doing this for *Honey*.

She wet her lips. "Are we—are we risking it?"

"What's life without a little risk?" Honey grinned again, and Sadie could almost convince herself the nervousness Honey was hiding was a natural extension of the excitement. That nothing bad would happen tonight.

Honey held up a pinkie.

Sadie rolled her eyes, but hooked her own pinkie around Honey's. Then she stilled, listening for heartbeats close enough to see them. There were none, just birds and beetles and a soft spring wind.

Sadie darted forward, fast enough to blur, and pressed a kiss to Honey's cool mouth.

chapter
two

THREE HOURS LATER, they were in an alley.

"Practically a date," Honey said brightly as she leaned against a grimy brick wall. "How many romantic moments have we had in alleyways?"

"Your idea of romance and mine are different." Sadie's jaw twitched. Her sharp gaze was trained on the dark mouth of the alleyway. The streetlight beyond the alley had gone out. If Honey was human, she'd be straining to see. As it was, she could pick out every split end in Sadie's thin black hair.

Music bled from a bar across the street. Honey sang along under her breath. "*Fun, hot, hungry.* Good motto for tonight."

Sadie didn't answer. She was perfectly still. Predator still. It was depressing. Tonight was supposed to be *fun*, a way to run away from their troubles before real life came rushing back in. Honey wanted to give Sadie some fun memories before dropping the whole college situation on her. Honey's dream college acceptance letter sat innocently among her emails, tucked in between a message from her mom about wearing sandals in dorm showers and a spam email that promised riches and fame in exchange for her credit card details.

Congratulations, and welcome to the University of California, Berkeley. You have been admitted for the fall semester of 2022 to the College of Natural Resources...

She had two weeks to accept the offer. She'd told everyone she had. She just hadn't...made it capital-O official. She needed to talk to Sadie first. Tell her she wasn't totally sold on college, and could they talk about it some more? Of course, if she didn't do it soon, the decision would be made for her.

Honey sidled up to Sadie, tweaking a belt loop in Sadie's tattered jeans. "Hey, maybe we should do *this* for spring break."

"What," Sadie said, her gaze still locked on the alleyway entrance. "Cruise around random cities, eating people?"

"Drinking," Honey corrected. "*Eating* makes it sound like we're killing people."

Sadie said nothing. Guilt flickered across her face, which was stupid. *Honey* was the serial killer—she'd killed every member of The Bleeding Bastards except for the bassist who sired her, plus Elijah at the start of the school year. Sadie'd had a few close calls when it came to ending someone's life, but—other than the drummer of The Bleeding Bastards, who had it coming—she never closed the deal. She had no reason to look so freaked out. She didn't even remember almost killing Summer and Ken's dad in the first week of school. Honey was the one who had to live with those memories—Mr. Lu screaming, Sadie hissing and clawing the whole time Honey dragged her out of the woods, her eyes solid black.

Honey shook the memory away and bit Sadie's arm through her flannel shirt. Blunt teeth, like when they were kids.

"Ow," Sadie said. But it shook that guilty look off her face, replacing it with fond exasperation.

Honey released her arm. "Everything will be fine. Don't be a drama queen. Can I drive on the way back?"

Sadie laughed like Honey had smacked the noise out of her. "You wish."

"Come on! I'll treat Steve-van right. I'll even remember to turn off the parking brake."

"Oh, wow," Sadie drawled. "When you say it like *that*—"

She stopped. There was a man coming down the street. Alone, like they wanted. He stunk of cigarettes and gin. He was humming along to the song drifting across the street from the smoky club: *fun, hot, hungry... come and take a bite if you're big enough...*

Honey tried to catch Sadie's eye, but Sadie was back in predator mode. Limbs perfectly still, gaze focused on the alleyway the man was about to walk past. Her eyes were already black. Fangs swelled underneath her lips.

"Take a chill pill," Honey told her. "We have to lure him in first."

She waited for Sadie to make fun of her for using a phrase from 2000s movies. It didn't come. Sadie's fingers twitched, ready to tear the guy to ribbons.

Honey stepped in front of her, plastering on an easy smile. "Remember the deal, crazy-eyes? I'll be the pretty little light on the anglerfish. You be the teeth. *Alllll* the way back there."

Sadie blinked. It was for Honey's benefit, to convince her she wasn't totally losing herself to the hunger. They didn't do the blinking thing so much these days.

Honey took Sadie's chin. "Hey. You can go first."

Finally, Sadie's gaze flickered to her. "You sure?"

"I'm sure. Just a taste, right?" Honey waited for Sadie to nod, a small, sharp movement against Honey's palm. Then she dropped her hand and sashayed up to the mouth of the alleyway, propping her hip against the bricks.

The man stumbled into view. He was in his midtwenties, stubble dark and uneven around his mouth. His t-shirt was festooned with that beer company from *The Simpsons*. His cigarette was almost finished, dangerously close to burning his fingers.

Honey cleared her throat. "Hey, you. Got a light?"

The man turned. His bleary gaze caught on the tight dress straining around Honey's soft hips, the sharp plunge of her neckline.

"Huh?"

Honey nodded at his cigarette. "Looking for a light. Got one I can borrow?"

He nodded, scrabbling for his jacket pocket. Then he hissed, tossing away his cigarette and sucking hard on his fingers. The cigarette had burned down, leaving two shiny burns where he'd clutched it.

Honey pouted. "Owie. Come here, let me look at that."

He blinked. He smiled, dopey and confused, but he still followed her. Of course he did. He was four inches taller than her, he was older, he was wasted and on top of the world. Nothing could touch him.

"You really shouldn't smoke," he slurred as he followed her into the dark alley. "'S a bad habit."

Honey tossed a grin over her shoulder. "I'm all about bad habits, baby."

He chuckled. The confusion was still there, but his survival instincts were undercut by the gin in his system and how short Honey's dress was. He still hadn't asked why Honey didn't have a cigarette.

Honey stopped. Sadie stood at the very back, hidden in the dark. If she had all her mind, she would be mouthing Honey's terrible lines mockingly. But she didn't have her mind. She was being eaten up by the hunger.

Honey's heart sank. This wasn't going to be fun. This was going to be yet another thing they would try to forget.

Honey thought about calling the whole thing off.

But when it came to Go Big Or Go Home, Honey never liked going home.

She turned. The guy had a new cigarette out, fumbling at his lighter.

"We could share," he offered. "I'm into bad habits, too."

"Good," Honey said quietly.

He cursed, shaking his lighter. "Sonofabitch won't—"

Sadie streaked out of the dark, so fast even Honey couldn't keep track. Sadie was a blur of pale skin and paler fangs, eyes liquid black as she shoved him hard into the bricks, wrenched his head back, and sank her teeth into his neck.

He screamed.

Honey winced. She waited for Sadie to cover his mouth and muffle the horrified shrieks streaming out of his mouth, but Sadie's hands stayed where they were: fisted in his jacket and his hair, holding him in place against the wall.

Just a taste, Honey had told her. Sadie had nodded. She'd wanted to mean it, Honey had seen it in her eyes. But there had been something bigger in her eyes, and they both knew it.

Honey cleared his throat. "Babe? Venom time?"

The guy screamed louder. There were no fun venom endorphins sneaking into his bloodstream, blissing him out. This was just pain, pure and simple.

Honey scooped up a trashcan lid from the concrete. "Hey. Babe. If you don't stop I'm gonna smack the shit out of you with this trashcan lid."

The guy's scream dwindled. His punches—clumsy and flailing against Sadie's back—slowed. His eyelids fluttered. And still Sadie drank. Wet, desperate noises as she sucked on his neck, tearing his skin even deeper. Blood dripped down his collar, soaking his Simpsons shirt.

"Come on," Honey sighed. She brought the trashcan lid down on Sadie's head. Not *too* hard—a warning shot.

Sadie stayed fixed in place, growling into the guy's throat.

The man moaned. His eyelids fluttered. Still no venom making him docile. He was passing out.

"Oookay." Honey reared back and took a running jump, slamming the trashcan lid directly into the side of Sadie's skull.

Sadie stumbled back, her fangs ripping from the man's skin. Another animalistic noise spilled out of her, and she raised black and angry eyes toward Honey. Her lips curled back in a snarl, her chin wet with blood.

The man sagged down the wall, moaning.

Yay, Honey thought. *Not dead.*

Sadie's head whipped around. She bent in a crouch.

Not dead yet, Honey corrected, and leapt. She caught Sadie in midair, slamming her into the bricks next to the man crumpled on the ground.

"Hey," Honey barked, grabbing the hands that

swiped at her. "No going feral on a fun night out! *Bad* girlfriend!"

Sadie's snarl trailed off. She blinked.

"There we go," Honey coaxed. "You coming back? Huh? Come back to me, Sadie."

Sadie stopped struggling. She blinked again, green filtering back into her eyes.

"That's right," Honey whispered. "Come all the way back."

Sadie clenched her eyes shut. When she opened them, they were all green, and she was Sadie again. *Her* Sadie, all split ends and worn flannel and baggy jeans. Even half a monster. Even with blood in her mouth.

"Honey," she said, the word turning clear and sweet as her fangs faded into blunt teeth. She glanced over, grimacing at the man on the verge of passing out beside them. "*Crap.*"

"Crap," Honey agreed. She bent down, pressing a swift kiss to Sadie's unbloodied forehead. "Wet wipes in Steve-van. I'll take care of the rest."

Sadie stumbled up, smearing her hands over her red cheeks. "Hon—"

"Go *fast*," Honey told her.

For a second Sadie just stood there, shoulders rigid, watching with that same ravenous hunger the man's chest rise and fall. Then she shook her head and blurred out of the alleyway, hopefully toward the wet wipes sitting in the van's glovebox.

Honey turned to the man, who was on his hands and knees now. Blood was heavy in the air, Honey's fangs fighting to come out. She forced them back in her gums and bent down. She had work to do.

chapter
three

THE SILENCE WAS SUFFOCATING. Sadie was half convinced Honey drifted into a lane without indicating just so Sadie would comment on it.

"I learned from the best," Honey replied, like always. Then she tossed her hair so it arced straight into Sadie's face.

Sadie plucked a strawberry blonde strand from her lip. "Did you heal him?"

"Sure did. Called an ambulance, too." Honey drummed her bare nails on the steering wheel. They were slightly too long, just like her leg hair was forever a little prickly. Anytime she trimmed them, they went right back to how she was the day she got turned. Sometimes Sadie caught her looking at pixie cuts and mohawks longingly. Honey loved her long hair, but being trapped with one hair length for eternity wasn't an exciting prospect. Still —better than being trapped with this insatiable hunger forever.

It's not forever, Honey always told her. *It hasn't even been a full year. Wait for it to settle.*

Like they had any other option.

Sadie shoved the hunger to the back of her mind. The drunk guy's blood wasn't enough. Not nearly enough. Maybe if she'd drained *all* of him...

She shuddered, focusing on the leather car seat, worn and scratchy underneath her. The peach deodorant neither of them needed but both of them wore. Anything but the memory of that man's neck opening under her teeth as she bit deep, but not deep enough. *Never* deep enough.

"You didn't get to eat," she pointed out.

"We'll stop for a deer on the way." Honey flashed her a mild smile. She was distracted, her worry finally peeking through. She always pretended she wasn't worried, but it would bleed through after Sadie screwed up yet again.

Sadie squirmed. "Sorry."

"It's fine!" Honey reached for the radio. "What do you think is on at eleven p.m. in this teeny town—"

"It's NOT fine," Sadie yelled, loud enough that Honey startled and dropped her hand from the radio. "I nearly killed Mr. Lu! I nearly kill everyone we bite during these road trips out of town. I walk around all day trying not to murder our classmates, and you *know* how hard they make it, I can hear all the shit they say about me. If I have to listen to Britney talk about how I smell *one* more time—"

Honey groaned. "You don't even *smell* anymore. We don't sweat!"

"I know!" Sadie pressed her forehead to the window, the coolness of the glass meeting her newly warm skin. She only stayed warm a few hours after feeding. "Any word from Milly about a cure?"

Honey hummed in a pitch not accessible to humans. "Still just killing me! So unless you want—"

"Shut up." Sadie unhooked her phone from the mount on the dashboard. No more need for Google Maps, it was a straight ride home from here. "Does Clarissa have any news on your sire?"

"Nope." Honey chewed her cheek, brown eyes gleaming dark in the dim light as she stared out at the road. *Another reason I hate driving,* she had told Sadie in those painstaking hours of teaching her on the back roads, *is that I always have to look at the stupid road. When I'm a passenger princess I get to look at you.* She was usually looking at Sadie as much as she could: she'd start with glances while they were talking, then the talk would run long and the looks would follow until Sadie was screaming at her to please, *please* look at the road before she totaled the van.

Honey wasn't looking at Sadie now. She sucked in a breath, another telltale sign: they only breathed when there was a point. Honey breathed when she wanted to sigh or laugh or when she was stressed. She looked pretty damn stressed.

"So," she said. "Um."

She drummed faster on the steering wheel.

Sadie's still heart clenched. Honey had been doing this a lot in the last few weeks: she'd start to tell her something, then stop. Sadie was two more attempts away from shaking it out of her. If there was a sword of Damocles hanging over her head, let it fall already.

"I wanted to talk about—" Honey frowned, staring at a car as it approached from the other direction. "Huh."

"What?"

Honey pointed. "Isn't that Alexander's car?"

Sadie twisted to watch a silver Beemer streak past. It was going too fast for any human to see details of the driver, but Sadie caught blonde hair and the vague shape of a guy in the front seat.

"Could be," Sadie said.

"It is," Honey said. "Same number plate."

"You know his number plate?"

Honey gave her an exasperated look. "Number plates are easy to remember," she scoffed, like that was a normal thing to say. Fondness curled in Sadie's chest.

"Maybe he's starting his spring break early," Honey suggested, and shot Sadie a grin. "Or following his looooove."

"He doesn't *like* me," Sadie argued.

"Ugh. People like you, bitch. Get over it." Honey jumped as her phone buzzed in her pocket. "Shit, that's my Google alert. Grab it? I have to keep my hands at ten and two or the van will spontaneously explode."

"I never said that." Sadie wriggled her fingers into Honey's jeans pocket and pulled out the phone. "It's Clarissa. She's sent us an article."

"Shit," Honey hissed. "Read it out."

"Uh, the headline's..." Sadie scrolled. "*Bassist from massacred indie band spotted in North Carolina*. He was in a bodega...buying bleach. Cool. Not creepy. Wait, there's a photo."

The picture loaded. It was grainy, taken on a crappy cellphone, and the angle was off. The photographer didn't want to be noticed. Despite this, the bassist's beady eyes were fixed right on the camera. He wore a dirty hoodie and sweatpants. His face was paler than usual and his hair stuck to his forehead.

"Hungry," Sadie murmured. She cleared her throat. "*The fan favorite of many true crime podcasts has been sighted buying bleach in a bodega in Fester, NC. Mystery surrounds the only survivor of The Bleeding Bastards. The band—sans our favorite bassist—was found chopped to pieces in a bathroom before one of their own gigs...*blah, blah."

"Anything about us?"

"Still no." Sadie minimized the article and tapped into Google Maps.

"Aw." Honey sighed, like they hadn't gone through eight kinds of shit when their town briefly believed they might have something to do with The Bleeding Bastards murders. "I wanna be a cryptid. How far?"

"Give me five seconds. God." Sadie waited for it to

load. The internet was slower than her speedy vampire fingers. "North Carolina is...nine hours."

"Easy. Do we want to stop in at Milly's? She's not totally on the way, but we can detour—"

"So we're going?"

Honey twisted to give her an incredulous look.

Sadie gave her one back. "What? We chased him at Thanksgiving, and we didn't come up with shit."

"So what, we let it go? We had two weeks in between finding the lead and chasing it. Spring break starts in two days, and I don't know about you, but I'd rather chase a lead and come up with shit than sit around for a week watching *Gilmore Girls* with you for the millionth time." Honey held out her pinkie. "You in?"

Sadie eyed her pinkie, so soft and familiar. "Cooper might fire me for taking time off without notice."

"So? You're quitting in a few months anyway." Honey wiggled her finger, and Sadie thought of hooks, meat, hungry fish. She curled her pinkie around Honey's. Even before she looked up and saw Honey's warm gaze not focused anywhere near the road, she knew what Honey was thinking: *To death and beyond, I vow to thee. Kill or die or bury a body.*

Munson startled in the kitchen doorway.

"Jesus," he said, flicking on the kitchen light. "What are you doing loading dishes in the dark?"

Sadie shrugged, slotting another dish in the top tray.

Munson Greer scratched his stomach through his threadbare shirt. Her dad still didn't know she was a vampire. If she was lucky, he'd never know. If she was *really* lucky, that would be because they found a cure, and not because she cut off all contact and went to live as a vampire hermit. Not that she'd actually do that. She joked about it with Honey, but if she stayed like this another ten years, she'd have to tell him. He'd be fine with it. Well—not *fine*. But he wouldn't take out the pitchforks. He'd make stiff jokes about coffins and not ask leading questions.

But for now, he was oblivious. Like he was about most things Sadie-related.

He squinted at the digital clock on the oven. "It's one a.m. You're still up?"

She shrugged again. Even before she was a vampire, she stayed up half the night, but she did it in her room, where he didn't notice. She had never told him how bad her drinking got. As long as she didn't drink directly in front of him, he hadn't noticed. She'd been hoping it would be the same with vampirism, and so far she'd been right: spots of blood on her clothes, lifting the TV like it was a handbag, never eating—all these things got a strange look, if anything. Then he'd go back to whatever he was doing.

Munson reached past her and closed the dishwasher. "Go to bed."

"Going." Sadie squeezed past him, her shoulders drooping at the idea of another night cooped up in her room seeing how fast she could find the Wikipedia entry for pineapple if she started on a random celebrity's page.

Munson cleared his throat. Sadie listened to the spit moving in his mouth.

"Hey," he said. "You still following Honey to college next year?"

Sadie paused halfway down the hall. Other than Honey's mom, Munson was the only one they'd told about their plans for next year.

"That's the plan," she said. "Why?"

He shrugged. The movement was stiff. He'd injured it in a climbing accident when he was Sadie's age, back when he used to go out and do things.

"Dunno how I feel about you following a girl across state lines when she doesn't even acknowledge you exist in the supermarket."

Sadie groaned. "Dad. That was *one* time. And I didn't acknowledge her, either! That was all you, being weird!"

He scratched his head, avoiding her eyes. The kitchen light hitting his back made him look like he was only half there. "I just don't get it. You two were thick as thieves a few years back. Now you're friends again, but you're not...I just don't get it. Keeping it a secret."

"It's not a big deal," Sadie tried. "It's just...easier. Until school ends. With everything that happened at the start of the year..."

"Right." Munson scratched his uneven stubble. "Still stupid they ever thought you were tangled up in that."

"We were tangled," Sadie pointed out. "That creep tangled us in it."

They avoided each other's eyes. Neither of them brought up Elijah, the guy who had crashed Honey's ex's birthday party and tried to kill them both.

Sadie tugged at her bob, which had stayed the exact same length since Honey turned her. "I'm going on a trip," she said before he could say anything. "Me and Honey. Over spring break."

He blinked blearily. "Where?"

"Just...around. Seeing the sights."

"You left for Thanksgiving as well." He scratched again at his worn shirt, which he'd owned since before she was born. "Didn't get to carve the turkey with you."

Sadie didn't see why it mattered. They'd barely done Thanksgiving in years—last year was the first time since mom left that he'd suggested an actual turkey instead of Chinese food.

"I'm a wild young thing," Sadie said. "Gotta go see what's out there."

He huffed. "Sure. I guess."

Sadie waited.

He made a noise like he was going to say more, but then he nodded and gestured down the hall. "Night," he said.

She nodded and continued down the hall. She was almost at his bedroom door when he called down to her: "Doing stuff is a fool's game."

She turned back. He was still in the kitchen doorway,

a crooked smile on his face. It was rigid, but weirdly hopeful. Like he wanted things to be nice for them in these last few months of her living under his roof. He was making an effort, like their mom always asked him to. It wasn't much—a smile and an awkward conversation—but suddenly Sadie wanted to tell him all of it. *Dad, I'm a vampire. It's bad. Last week I almost bit you because you stood too close when you were making coffee. I almost killed a guy tonight. Again!*

"Much safer to stay at home," Sadie said instead, and ducked into her bedroom.

chapter
four

HONEY DID her best to tune out the cafeteria chatter. She was getting better at it. It helped that she'd been tuning out Summer for years. Not all the time—just when she got boring. Which was annoyingly often.

She stared down at her phone. Every time she looked at her acceptance email she started imagining her future: she'd get her first degree and then do postgrad, get a Masters in something that allowed her to work in conservation or wildlife management or go all in on entomology. And then...then *what*? If she was still a vampire, there was an age limit where she could pass her looks off as severe babyface. She'd have to disappear, and then all her degrees would be useless. She knew how to get a fake ID; she didn't know how to get a fake *degree*.

But if they found her sire and she became human again—the world was her oyster. Degrees out the wazoo. Or if her scholarships ran out and her student debt got unmanageable, she'd go straight into work. Travel. See strange sights and stranger animals. Do studies, make a name for herself, turn into one of those weird, hot old ladies with a cool house and too many pets.

And Sadie...

Honey glanced over at the empty table in the corner where Sadie usually sat, her tray filled with food she'd dump in the trash on her way out.

This was where Honey's imagination tripped up. They could maybe cure Honey's vampirism, but there was no cure for Sadie's unless she killed her girlfriend.

Honey's jaw worked. Maybe she wouldn't kill her sire. Maybe they'd be stuck like this together, forever. They could carve out a life. It'd be small, and they'd have to move every ten years once the babyface excuses got old, or if Sadie went feral and killed someone, or if they got caught sucking someone's blood in a dark alleyway—

"Honey! Hey!" Fingers snapped in front of Honey's face.

Honey's hand flew out. Too fast.

Britney stared at the iron grip Honey had on her wrist. She had come up to the table while Honey was deep in thought—the first time she'd come near Honey in months. She'd spent senior year at Ken's table, idly tracing the scar on his arm from Elijah's knife.

"Um," Britney said. She traded a panicked look with Summer, who shrugged helplessly.

"Ninja reflexes," Honey blurted, and dropped Britney's moisturized arm. "Did you have a reason for coming over, or did you just want to annoy me?"

Britney blinked. She sucked in her cavernous cheeks, something she only did when she wanted people to know she was displeased. "I said your name *three* times before you zoned back in from whatever dimension you were lost in. Sorry for bringing you back to the real world."

She gave Summer another desperate look.

Summer fidgeted with her hair. "We were, um, talking about a road trip. Together. All three of us?"

Honey gave her a wry look. She wasn't an idiot. She knew Summer and Britney still hung out. She just didn't want to know about it.

"For old time's sake," Summer continued with a hopeful smile.

Britney scoffed. "I don't know why I let you talk me into this. She's not coming, babe. She's already dumped me, no way she's going to be friends with *you* after high school."

Summer glared at her. "Brit!"

"What? I say we don't even sign her yearbook. She's always treated us like we're second priority."

"I'm right here, Brit." Honey scooted back in her chair, making the other girls wince at the chair legs screeching against the linoleum. She looked over at Summer. "Is this because I didn't come to your birthday party?"

"No," Summer started, but Britney was already talking over her.

"You said you were sick! And then Hannah H. saw you walking around town at two in the morning!"

Britney spared a cautious look around the room, then lowered her voice. "I don't know why you even *bother* hanging with Summer anymore. Just go and hang with Sadie, like you obviously *want* to. Go be weirdos together."

Summer didn't dare meet Honey's eyes. Honey didn't blame her. She was sure her face was doing something truly dangerous, judging by how anxious Britney looked, even as she tried to hide it.

Honey leaned back to look at Britney's usual table. Ken was sitting with his back to them, stroking the scar Elijah had given him at his birthday party.

Honey turned back and beamed, enjoying how it made Britney startle. She leaned back hard in her chair, far enough that the girls eyed it worriedly.

"Good thing I can make weirdo hot," Honey whispered, and tipped backward.

Summer gasped. Britney made a noise like a pot boiling over.

Before she could plummet to the floor, Honey's hand shot out and grabbed the edge of the table. She pulled herself back up effortlessly, chair sliding back into place on all fours.

"Ladies." Honey tinkled a wave at their gawking faces. On her way out she glanced over at Sadie's empty table. At first she'd thought Sadie was late for her lunch period, but it was almost over and Sadie was nowhere to be seen. She'd been staying home from school a lot lately.

Being around people is too much, she said sometimes.

Honey didn't know if she meant *people* or *tasty, tasty humans.* Sometimes it included Honey. She'd ask if she could come over and make out, or watch *Gilmore Girls,* or even just sit in the room while Sadie lay under her covers—the most low-effort of hangouts—and Sadie would only reply the next day.

Got busy, she'd say. The stupidest and most obvious lie. Sadie was rarely busy unless it was with Honey. But what was she supposed to say—she was asleep?

Honey's glance became a stare. She was still staring at the empty cafeteria table when she smacked into Alexander White in all his polo-shirt-clad glory, the force of her solid frame sending him straight into the ground.

"Ow," he wheezed, staring up at the ceiling. "Alright."

Honey bent over him. "You really need to watch where you're going."

She grabbed him by the shoulders and hauled him up.

"Wow," he said, looking over her curvy figure. "Stronger than you look."

Are you just going to stand there repeating your lines, Honey wanted to ask. But she didn't want him to know she was listening with Sadie. She smiled, cocking her head in that way that made guys think they had the upper hand.

"I'm all muscle," she chirped, and flexed a soft arm. "Invisible, obviously. Not like *you.*"

She reached out and squeezed his bicep. It flexed

under her hand, and Honey had to stop her eyebrows from bumping up. He was pretty buff under those polo shirts.

"Anyway," she said, letting go. "Byeee!"

He stepped in front of her, smiling that same polo-shirt-catalog smile he'd given Sadie. "Do you have plans for spring break?"

Another frisson of panic churned in her stomach. *Maybe he's just clumsy*, she told herself. *Maybe he does want to sleep with Sadie. Maybe he just went out for a drive. Maybe we don't have to worry about this guy at all.*

Her gut told her otherwise. Elijah had said there would be more coming. Why not a sophomore with muscles and a too-slick smile?

She fixed up another grin. "You know, I thought I saw your car on the road into town last night. I assumed you'd taken off on spring break early. I was surprised to see you at school."

He blinked, brow wrinkling in polite confusion. "I didn't leave town last night."

Gotcha. Honey's lips pursed in victory. Something was *up* with this guy. That was *his* car, proud and shining in the parking lot every day, *his* blonde hair flashing past on the road.

Alexander's wide shoulders twitched. His smile faltered. Then it came right back, only a little strained. "What were *you* doing, driving out of town?"

"Driving lessons," Honey said brightly.

They stared at each other. She could smell the sweat under his armpits.

Honey doubled down on her grin. "Road trip!"

"Sorry?"

"For spring break," Honey explained. "What about you, what's little Alex doing?"

His nostrils flared, annoyance flickering over his features. Exactly the kind of reaction Honey had been hoping with his nickname. If he hated people calling him Alex instead of Alexander, he had to hate a modifier. Especially something like *little*. She could already feel his ego quivering with rage.

His teeth tightened. Less a smile than a grimace.

"That depends," he told her.

"On what?"

"On what you say next."

chapter
five

ALEXANDER WHITE SHOWED up at the Italian place at exactly seven p.m., a red flower pinned to his lapel and a small sports bag dangling from his wrist. He looked nervous behind his smile, like he really was just a sixteen-year-old on a first date.

"I hope we're wrong," Honey whispered as she watched him walk up to the front desk. "I hope he's just a dumbass and this whole night can be an exercise in how to make fun of a sophomore who thought he had a chance asking out a hot senior."

She didn't look over to where Sadie was tucked away at a corner table, pretending to examine a menu.

"Fingers crossed," Sadie whispered.

Honey crossed her fingers under the table, waving as Alexander spotted her. He waved back and started toward her, his eager jog becoming a cool, casual walk.

"I actually reserved us a table," he told her as he

arrived. "Is that alright? I'd hate to mess up their bookings."

Honey looked around the mostly empty restaurant. It was a new place, but this was a small town on a Thursday night. They wouldn't get slammed.

"Sure," Honey said brightly. "Lead the way."

He led them to a table in the corner. He even pulled out a seat, letting Honey sit before sliding into his own chair. It was an objectively worse table—they could barely see the windows, and they were right next to the kitchen, the scent of garlic and oil and tomato spilling out and making Honey want to weep with how much she missed human food.

Another thing they were right next to: Sadie Greer.

Sadie held the menu between them like a shield, bending low like she was examining the calorie counts. This place listed the calories with each meal, which the girls had complained about before Alexander showed up. *Calorie-counting is devil math,* Sadie had said darkly, and Honey had been struck with how much she wanted to go over there and shoot the shit with her secret girlfriend, forgo Alexander entirely, screw their plan. And then Alexander had shown up, and the suspicion in her gut had gone haywire once more.

Alexander rolled his shoulders against the wall, his chair backed up right against the polished wood. He set his sports bag under the table.

"Just came from the gym," he explained. "You look great."

"I know." Honey preened. She was hot with no effort, and she'd spent forty minutes getting ready for this. "You, too. What kind of flower is that?"

He touched the small flower tucked into his lapel. It was shaped kind of like jasmine, with sparse red petals gleaming against his white button-down. The stem was an even darker red, covered in tiny thorns.

"I don't know," he said, too fast. "It was just lying around the house. Do you like it?"

"Oh my god, I *love* it. But it can't be comfortable—all those thorns." She reached out to touch it.

He grabbed her wrist.

Sadie made a noise under her breath.

Honey's smile froze in place. She eyed Alexander's flimsy human fingers. She could break his grip in an instant. She could break his whole *hand*, which was gripping her arm so hard his knuckles went white.

Then, just as fast as he'd reached out, he released her.

"Sorry," he said. "I just—it's a good luck charm. In my family. I'm not supposed to let anyone else touch it."

Honey leaned forward on her elbows. "Yeah? Hoping to get lucky?"

He choked on a laugh, his gaze going anywhere but the cleavage she'd just put on display. Honey pushed her hair behind her ears, using the movement to sneak a glance at Sadie, who was peering at her over her menu. Honey resisted the urge to shoot her a wink.

"So," Alexander said as a waiter poured water into their glasses. "So what's happening on this road trip?"

"The usual chaos." Honey gave him a playful grin, imagining Sadie's eyeroll.

"Yeah? People usually go on road trips for a reason. Getting to college, or seeing family." Alexander paused to smile in thanks at the waiter. He was still smiling when he continued, "Following a band."

Sadie made another noise.

Honey bit the inside of her cheek, waiting for Alexander to meet her gaze again. It took a second, Alexander staring down into his glass as he drank, finally resurfacing once the silence had stretched long enough. He looked at her like he was daring her to ask.

"You're sixteen," Honey said. "Right? You just had your birthday party."

"I did. I was sad you didn't come."

Honey giggled. "You're ballsy for a sixteen-year-old."

"What, for asking you out?" Alexander shook his head. "You're not that scary."

The waiter came back, notepad in hand.

"Hi," Alexander said, all smooth, like this wasn't the weirdest dinner Honey ever had. He didn't even look at the menu. "I'll have the steak."

"I'll get the risotto. Thanks so much." Honey waited until the waiter was out of earshot. "Steak at an Italian place?"

"Steak's always a safe bet." He took another mouthful of water, not looking away this time. He nodded at Honey's glass. "Have a sip, it's sparkling."

Honey made a face. "I hate sparkling." It was even true, once upon a time.

"Your loss. So, what college are you going to?"

Honey fought the urge to look over at Sadie again. Her phone sat heavily in her jumpsuit pocket, the acceptance letter lying in wait, along with that looming deadline.

"Berkeley."

"Smart choice," he said. "What do you want to major in?"

"I haven't decided," Honey lied. She wasn't telling anyone in this small town she wanted to get a job where she dealt with weird insects. That wasn't for them to know. When she moved, she could start fresh. Become the kind of person who could have that kind of life.

"What about you?" she asked. "What's little Alex doing with his life?"

"I'm—" Alexander paused as the waiter stopped by their table, placing a napkin-wrapped set of utensils in front of him. He nodded in thanks, sliding a steak knife out of the folds and flipping it expertly around his fingers.

"I'm going into the family business," he said, spinning the knife deftly in his hand.

At the next table, Sadie whispered behind her menu. "*Honey.*"

Honey glanced at her. Alexander looked with her, just a second before his head jerked back toward Honey.

But it was enough: there was no surprise on his face when he saw Sadie crouched behind her menu.

"What's—" Honey smothered a giggle. She couldn't help it. This whole thing was so *stupid*. "What's the family business?"

"Pest control," Alexander said dryly. The knife made another controlled arc around his hand. Maybe he'd stab her right here at the table and Honey wouldn't have to come up with an excuse to not eat her food after all.

"Hot," Honey managed. She eyed the knife. She'd only had a few run-ins with real silver since becoming a vampire. It burned, and it took longer to heal.

"You know," Honey continued. "You really don't look much like him."

He shrugged, still spinning the knife.

Honey lowered her voice. "You know he was going to kill some innocent YouTuber. Right? *And* he stabbed my ex. He didn't care how many people got hurt as long as he killed us."

"He was on the hunt," Alexander said briskly. "And when you're on the hunt, anything—"

The knife slipped. Alexander's eyes widened in shock as he fumbled, trying to catch it. The blade sliced into his palm. Blood splattered onto the tablecloth.

"Oh," he said, voice hitching as the red stain grew. "O-okay."

Saliva pooled in Honey's mouth. Her teeth sharpened, her nails digging into her skirt-clad knees hard enough to tear a human's skin. She'd drained a deer dry last night, but she hadn't had human blood since she turned Sadie. The hunger was instinctual and incredible.

She turned around just in time to see Sadie's chair topple to the ground and a black blur launch toward Alexander.

Honey caught her in midair, momentum plunging them into the table. Wood cracked and splintered, Alexander reeling back with a shout. A nearby waitress stumbled back and spilled a jug of water down a man's shirt.

Sadie snarled, rearing up to grab at Alexander's slacks. Her eyes were black, lip curled back to show her fangs.

"Nope," Honey snapped, dragging her back by her waist. "Bad Sadie! Get off!"

Sadie twisted, digging her teeth into Honey's shoulder.

Honey shrieked. She wasn't the only one—more people were shouting now, getting up from their chairs. Someone pulled out their phone.

"Don't call the cops," Honey shouted at them. "Everything's fine."

She wrenched Sadie back by her hair, teeth ripping out of her shoulder. Black blood streamed from the bite mark. Sadie struggled, straining to get to Alexander, who was cursing as he tugged the stubborn zipper of his sports bag.

"Everything's fine," Honey yelled again as another person got out their phone. She held Sadie tightly by her hair, forcing her face toward her. "Hey. *Hey*. Look at me. This can't happen. We're already gonna have to do damage control, and it will get *so* much worse if you eat him."

Sadie's growling trailed off uncertainly.

"There we go," Honey whispered, wiping a shred of table wood off Sadie's cheek. "Coming back to me?"

Black leached out of Sadie's eyes, leaving that beautiful green Honey knew so well.

Her mouth opened.

An arrow burst out of her chest. They both stared at it. Black blood was running down her shirt and onto her jeans.

"Ow," Sadie said weakly, and collapsed against Honey. Alexander came into view behind her, holding a silver crossbow in front of him. It was huge and sleek, with a diamond carved cleanly into the handle. His bloody finger was on the trigger.

"Crap," Honey spat, and pulled Sadie out of the way of another bolt. Pain exploded in her shoulder. An arrow had hit her, piercing all the way to the bone.

Honey shrieked and dropped Sadie on the restaurant carpet.

"THIS IS ALL PERFORMANCE ART," she yelled, black tears streaming down her face as someone across the room held a phone up to their ear. "NOBODY CALL THE COPS!"

Alexander reloaded the crossbow. Honey looked at Sadie, crumpled and groaning on the floor with an arrow in her chest that would burn Honey to touch. Then she sprinted at Alexander, making sure to keep her speed normal. It meant he had time to swear and aim for another shot. Honey dodged the arrow as it lodged into the carpet near her feet, and barreled into him.

"You're really gonna do this in front of *everybody*," she hissed, fighting through the pain to pin him down. He had one hand free, the hand with the crossbow in it.

"If we—ow!" She'd leaned too close. The black flower in his lapel dug thorns into her collarbone. The thorns didn't just pierce—they *burned*, like silver.

Honey leaned back, gritting her teeth. "If we went for a walk in one of our amazing, deserted parks, maybe you could get away with it. Here? You're screwed. Let me get us out of this."

He glared at her, his blue eyes full of hate. The crossbow poked clumsily into her side. If he pulled that trigger, the arrow would drive straight into her stomach.

Honey winced. "How about this? We die, you die, too. I can kill you before anyone can help."

Alex jeered. "You kill me, my family will tear you apart. They'll follow you wherever you go."

"Good luck finding us." Honey raised her head. The hushed whispering around them was getting louder. Someone yelled in the kitchen, someone else crouched behind the bar whispering details to the cops.

Honey yelled, "THIS IS AN AHEAD-OF-ITS-TIME WORK OF PERFORMANCE ART! YOU GUYS ARE A TERRIBLE AUDIENCE! GUY

BEHIND THE BAR, TELL THE COPS TO CHILL OUT!"

She ducked back down. "Look. I'm going to get up, you're going to tell everybody it's just a show—"

"I'll find you," Alex whispered. "You don't even know, do you? We have tracking spells, you *idiot*. I'll track you to the ends of the earth."

"Oh my god, shut *up*." Honey glanced up at Sadie's limp body across the restaurant. No breathing, no heartbeat. *She's not dead,* Honey told herself as anguish washed over her in a paralyzing wave. *The arrow is in the middle of her chest. It missed her heart.*

Alexander started, "We'll always—"

Honey slapped him. Alexander's indigent splutter turned into a grunt of pain as Honey pressed down on him with almost all her strength.

"You're annoyingly persistent," Honey told him. "So I'm going to tell you what we're really doing for spring break. We're going to kill our sire. Know what that does?"

Alexander frowned. "You want to be—"

"Un-vamped, yeah. We'll be human in one week. You can't kill vampires who are gonna be human in one week."

"But only one of you—"

"We'll kill him together," Honey lied. "It'll work. It's worked before."

Alexander struggled against her, his trapped arm moving uselessly. The crossbow jabbed harder into her side, silver ripping through the flimsy fabric of her dress. "If you think I'm going to just let you go off on a road trip—"

"Come with us," Honey said, keeping the wince out of her voice as silver burned into her stomach. "If you're so worried. If we aren't human at the end of spring break, you can do your best to kill us."

It wasn't a fix—not even close. Even if everything worked out, Sadie would still be a vampire. But it would buy them time to come up with something better.

Alex stared up at her, his face twisted in disbelief.

"Or I can just kill you now." Honey bared her fangs. "Live or die, little Alex. What's it gonna be?"

His face twisted harder at the condescending nickname. But finally it seemed to sink in: fear seeped through his hatred, the first real glimpse of fear since he'd brought out the crossbow.

"Live," he spat.

She patted his cheek. "Good choice."

chapter
six

SADIE WOKE UP NUMB.

Her mouth tasted like death, and not in a fun, bloody way. Her throat was so dry it hurt to swallow. She pried her eyes open and found she was lying in Steve-van's backseat, her blessed guitar shoved in the footwell beside her. It was dark outside. There was a hole in her chest.

She prodded at her torn shirt, stained with black blood. The wound didn't...*hurt*, exactly. It was like getting injured in a dream, a dull ache that you knew should be much worse.

"Gotta love those numbing vampy painkillers," came Honey's chirpy voice from outside her hazy vision. "He just had to take the silver out first."

"He?" Sadie mumbled.

"Me," came another voice, preppy and snarling.

Sadie looked up. Alexander White glared back at her from the passenger seat. He had a crossbow aimed at her face.

Sadie yelped, jerking up and grabbing her guitar, like she was actually going to smash him with it.

"It's fine," Honey yelled from the driver's seat. There was a spot of black on her chin and a pair of heart-shaped sunglasses sat low on her nose.

Sadie groaned, sifting through her groggy memories. She'd been in a restaurant, hiding behind a menu like an idiot in a B movie, watching Honey toy with Alexander. She remembered being nervous, planning exit strategies. Alexander started flipping a knife and talking about *family businesses*, and Sadie had been about to tell Honey to quit the whole thing. Then Alexander's knife slipped, and the world narrowed down into the sweet, irresistible blood spilling down his hand.

The rest was a blur: lunging, the table splintering, Honey holding her down. An arrow sticking out of her chest. Looking over as her vision tunneled to see Honey launch herself at Alexander and shove him to the ground, a silver bolt sticking out of her shoulder.

She looked up. Alexander was still scowling at her, the crossbow twitching like he wasn't sure if he wanted to level it at her or Honey. His hand was bandaged, a spot of red in the fabric. Dark. Tantalizing—

Sadie tore her gaze away. "What day is it?"

"Friday," Honey said. She drummed on the wheel, her erratic drumbeat giving away what her bored expression wouldn't. "I texted your dad. Told him you're fine, just passed out drunk after our party celebrating a performance well done."

"Performance?"

"I mean, I had to say *something*." Honey beamed at Alexander, her smile turning whip-mean when he glowered back at her. "I made him bow with me, back at the restaurant. Said you were just really focused on staying in character as I carried you out. It was a total maiden carry, it was super hot."

She tossed her hair. Alexander's hand twitched around the crossbow, like Honey's hair was a lethal weapon he needed to be careful of.

Sadie stared at him. "Why is he *here*?"

"I told him the plan. Kill our sire together, steal our humanity back. He insisted on coming with." Honey glanced in the rear-view mirror, her sharp smile hardening. "So now we have a road trip buddy. It'll be nice having a third pair of hands to kill that shithead, right?"

Her gaze met Sadie's in the mirror. Sadie knew that look. She knew all of Honey's looks. This was the look Honey gave her when she told their fifth grade teacher she found the hamster already dead.

I'm lying my ass off, the look said. *Go along with it.*

"Right," Sadie said slowly. "As long as he doesn't take the kill. It has to be us."

"At the same time," Alexander said. "I've never heard of that happening—"

Honey cut him off. "Milly will tell you all about it on

the way back. Unless you think *she's* lying, too, and this is all one big vampire conspiracy to screw you over."

Raindrops hit the windshield. Honey reached for the windscreen wipers and turned on the indicators instead. "Oops."

"Other side," Sadie reminded her, clutching her guitar. It felt like a lifetime since they had been in Milly Hart's house in Tennessee, where the strange gray-eyed woman had blessed the guitar as a defense against enemy vampires. What had her life turned into?

"I got it." Honey switched on the windshield wipers. "See? I'm an awesome driver. I have a license and everything."

"Because you flirted with the instructor to make him forgive your immediate fail."

"Who *actually* comes to a complete stop at a stop sign?"

Alexander watched the two of them with a bewildered expression. Sadie did her best to ignore him. If he was stuck in this van for the next week, he'd have to get used to the Honey-and-Sadie show.

Honey pulled the van over to the side of the road, the headlights illuminating the long grass.

Alexander snarled, jabbing the crossbow at her. "I didn't say you could—".

"We need to hunt." Honey slid her heart-shaped sunglasses off and folded them in one practiced click, ignoring the deadly weapon pointed at her chest. "Gotta fuel up if we want to heal up."

"I—"

Honey turned to him, eyes flashing black. "What are we gonna do, little Alex? We're injured. We're not going to abandon Steve-van, it's the most expensive thing Sadie owns. We can't run away, I'm going to college in a few months and I need to finish high school."

Alexander's jaw twitched. Water hit the roof, drizzle turning into proper rain.

Honey rolled her eyes. "Look, if you're just gonna sit there like a little bitch—"

"We'll come back," Sadie said. She sat up, wincing as the strange numbness flooded the rest of her torso. "We have no choice."

He glared at them. He looked tired, Sadie realized. Tired and stressed and *young*. He'd had his sixteenth birthday party last month. Everybody showed up on Monday laughing about how he yelled at someone for breaking a vase.

He lowered the crossbow. "If you're not back in twenty minutes, I start up a tracking spell."

"A *what*?"

"Tell you later," Honey said, and blurred out of the van to help Sadie into the rain.

Their injuries slowed them down, but not by much. They took down three deer, a fox, and a blackbird who had the bad sense to perch low in a tree. By the end of it they were both covered in blood from nose to neck. Rain drenched their slick bodies, running red and black into the forest floor.

"Free shower," Honey said over the thunder. "Who needs motels?"

Sadie flexed her bare feet against the dirt. They'd left their shoes in the van. Easier to hunt barefoot.

Honey scratched her injured shoulder. The arrow had pierced straight through her sleeve.

Sadie pulled at the ruined fabric. "You brought clothes, right?"

"He graciously allowed me to pack. I stopped at both our places." Honey ran a hand through Sadie's sodden hair and pulled her close. "Quit freaking out."

"I'm not freaking out," said Sadie, whose panic was winning out over the temporary relief of a successful hunt.

"You're totally freaking out, stop it. I have a fool-proof plan."

"Oh, a foolproof plan. What's your foolproof plan, Hon?"

Honey paused for dramatic effect. Sadie wanted to strangle her. Sadie wanted to cry in her arms. Sadie wanted to kiss her until the red ran out of their mouths.

Honey announced: "We make him like you."

Sadie waited for the actual plan. When Honey just kept staring at her, she groaned.

"No, it's great, he can't kill you if he's attached," Honey argued, brushing Sadie's wet hair off her fore-head. "Like you and that grass spider after I told you a bunch of facts about it. We need to endear you to him, and then he won't merc you after we kill the sire and you're still fangy."

Endear, Sadie mouthed. "What about his family?"

"He'll lie to them for us. Because he'll like you."

"That won't—people don't *like* me."

"And yet you have a super hot girlfriend who's obsessed with you."

Sadie chuckled, too exhausted to tease her about it. She was shaking. It happened sometimes after a decent feed. She still felt weak, even after all the animals she'd drained. The hole in her chest oozed black.

"It won't work," she argued.

"It's gonna have to. It's that or kill him and go on the run."

"No. You gotta go to college." Sadie slumped over to Honey and buried her face in her slick neck. "Wish you were human," she mumbled. "Never got to drink you."

"I know." Honey stroked her wet hair. "I miss biting you. You were the best thing I ever tasted."

They had a homicidal sixteen-year-old to get back to. A sire to kill. Clean clothes to change into. But they stayed there in that wet forest for a while longer, cleaning blood off each other before the rain could get to it.

chapter
seven

HONEY TAPED a bandage over the oozing hole in Sadie's chest.

"Totally normal looking," she assured Sadie as she buttoned the flannel shirt over it. "No one got stabbed here, officer."

Sadie made a face. Honey couldn't tell if it was from her lackluster attempts at making Sadie laugh or from the smell. Their motel room stunk like mold, and it was even stronger on their bed. They had two—a twin bed in one corner, a single bed in the other. Honey had called dibs on the twin bed as soon as they walked in. Alexander had given her a look like she was the biggest idiot in the world before dumping his sports bag on the single bed, and Honey had remembered all those mutters in the cafeteria about how Alexander wouldn't recognize a joke if it gave him a purple nurple.

"Shouldn't have even gotten a bed," he had mumbled. "Just wasting money."

Sadie tugged on her newly buttoned shirt collar, glancing at the closed bathroom door Alexander was lurking behind. "You couldn't have packed better clothes?"

"Aw, baby. You don't *have* better clothes," Honey said sweetly, smoothing the ratty flannel down. It was her softest shirt, worn only when Sadie needed to feel like she was being hugged at all times. Honey had torn her room apart to find it.

Sadie sat down on the stained bedsheets, dazed. Honey joined her. Twenty-four hours ago she had been cleaning blood off Sadie's face in Steve-van's backseat. Mostly with wet wipes, sometimes with her tongue.

"I can drive tomorrow," Sadie offered.

Honey snorted. "Sure. Want to give me a striptease on the hood, too? Either sounds equally stupid." She prodded Sadie's shirt, right over the bandage. By the time she'd buttoned the shirt over it, black goo was already bleeding through.

Sadie opened her mouth, ready to protest.

"You might not sleep, but you still need rest." Honey shuffled up the bed, weary in her bones. She missed sleep almost as much as food. "You're spending tomorrow lying in the backseat and charming the shit out of our resident psychopath in there."

She jerked her head toward the closed bathroom door.

Sadie groaned. It wasn't her usual *you're so annoying, why do I love you so much* groan. It was trying to be, but

54

her shoulders were too slumped, the noise too low for it to be anything other than true desperation.

Honey gritted her teeth. "Sadie. You just need to show him how awesome you are."

"I—"

"When we were kids you didn't bother being friends with anyone because you had me," Honey said over her. She took Sadie's face, stopping her from twisting away. "Then you turned into an asshole and no one *could* be friends with you because you were so dickish to them they gave up. I *know* the stoners tried befriending you, don't tell me they didn't. You never let people see the cool, fun, weird Sadie I know. If you did, you'd be *rolling* in friends."

Sadie made another face. Honey squished her cheeks until the look faded into mostly fond irritation.

"He wants to kill us," Sadie said, muffled by Honey's firm press.

"We'll be making friendship bracelets by the end of spring break," Honey said. "You'll—"

The bathroom door opened. The scent wafting out of it made their heads snap around.

Alexander stood rigid in the bathroom doorway, his hands in tight fists. The bandages around his injured hand were new—he'd bled in the bathroom. Honey could smell it under the noxious stench of cleaning fluids. He'd bled and he'd cleaned it up, and there was new blood on the hasty bandages. Not nearly as much as there had been at the restaurant. But enough.

Honey's teasing press around Sadie's jaw turned into a vice grip.

"I did a tracking spell," Alexander announced, voice thin as he crossed the room toward his bed. "Your sire's still in Fester. We're on the right track."

"Awesome," Honey said. She glanced at Sadie, who still had green eyes, not even a thread of black flickering through.

Sadie twitched her head in a nod. *I'm okay.* She kept her lips clamped shut, not daring to let any accidental intake of breath slip through.

Honey let go of her face. When she looked back at Alexander he was kneeling next to his bed, only visible from the neck up as he shuffled through the contents of his sports bag.

"Who's Milly?"

Honey paused. "What?"

"You've mentioned her three times, like I'm supposed to know who that is. Is she another vampire?"

"No," said Honey, watching him pull out a pair of pajama bottoms, a tank top, a crossbow, and two curved silver knives. "She's our magical advice guru. She helped us when we first turned. She's looking into other ways we can turn human if something...goes wrong. With the sire plan."

He paused in the middle of laying another knife on the bedspread. "There are no other ways. Is she stupid?"

"Are *you* stupid?" Honey snapped. Then she winced, nudging for Sadie to fix it. Sadie gave her a pointed look

—still straining to control herself, and Honey was the one she relied on when it came to talking to people anyway.

Talk, Honey mouthed at her. She checked he was busy counting his weird knives and continued, *Make him like you.*

Sadie gave her a scathing look to let her know exactly what she thought of that plan, but obliged. "We don't know that for sure. Maybe there is a way, it just hasn't been discovered yet."

"There isn't," Alexander replied, just as assured as before. He placed another silver knife down—small wicked curves and large bowies with serrated edges, all in one neat line on the thin motel bedspread. They were all pristine, lethally sharp, and had a small diamond carved into the wooden handles. Just like the crossbow, Honey noticed. Maybe it was a family thing.

"My family has been doing this for generations," he continued. "We'd know."

Sadie's lips thinned. "We have to *try*. If...if I get the kill while Honey's on the other side of the room, like, injured or something, we can't just throw up our hands like, *well, shit, I tried. Sucks for you, Hon. Have fun eating strangers in alleyways for the next hundred years*. We're not gonna just give up on each other. Honey's, like...my whole life."

She took a breath like she was about to say more. Then she clicked her mouth shut—because of the blood smell but also because she was embarrassed, if the pained look and averted gaze was anything to go by. Pained from the blood, looking away from the embarrassment of saying anything vulnerable, especially to someone she didn't know very well.

Honey tore her gaze away from Sadie's embarrassment to find Alexander ducking his head, resuming his knife-sorting. He'd been staring.

"Whatever," he muttered. "If you want to set yourself up for disappointment, go for it."

He straightened the last knife in the line, then brought out a small white cloth and started rubbing them down. Honey honestly couldn't tell if it was an intimidation tactic or if this was his regular nighttime routine, and he refused to give it up just because he was stuck in a motel room with two bloodthirsty seniors.

Honey pulled a smile on and stood. "You know what? I refuse to let this week be tense, boring or scary. It's spring break! Let's do *spring break* things. Let's do *road trip* things. Who's with me?"

They both stared at her. Honey pulled out her phone and started typing. "Okay, Google says there's a haunted theme park a few hours away. Oooh, world's largest collection of gay magnets, we have to see that."

"This is the most important week of your lives and you want to go see gay magnets," Alexander said slowly.

Honey waved at him. "If we have a vampire GPS, yeah! We can stretch this out. We can make it to Fester in —what, six hours? That's *nothing*. We have days and days to do spring break stuff."

"Like what?" Sadie asked, sounding reluctant to hear the answer.

Honey kept her smile intact as her mind raced. Since freshman year, spring break meant parties. But Alexander wasn't a party guy, Honey knew that much from her halfhearted participation in cafeteria chatter.

"So we can't get wasted," Honey started. "But we can do, like. Party stuff! Alex, truth or dare?"

"*Alexander*," he barked. "And I'm not *playing* with you. I'm cleaning my knives. Then I'm going to sleep for four hours. And if you aren't there when I wake up—"

"Jesus, unclench." Honey tried not to let actual irritation slip into her tone. She had to be *playfully* annoyed, to tease him in a *hot* way, not a grating way. She flopped back down on the bed, sprawled easily to display how effortlessly cool she was. *You could be like this, too,* she tried to convey with her relaxed sprawl. *Put the stupid crossbow away.*

"I know you're very dedicated," Honey tried. "But you're also sixteen. I remember the halcyon days of sixteen—"

"You're two years older than me," Alexander said flatly.

"And sixteen-year-olds want to have *fun*. So, Alexander: truth or dare?"

He glared at her, polishing a sickle knife with such swift, careful precision Honey almost wanted to applaud him for it. Maybe this *was* his usual bedtime routine.

"Once Honey decides you're playing, you're playing," Sadie advised. She shifted on the bed, arranging her stiff limbs in a pale imitation of Honey's carefree sprawl. "It's faster if you just go with it."

Honey cocked her head, beaming in a way that made most guys melt.

He glared harder. He slid his knives into a sheath, all of them strapped in one long line. At first Honey thought she'd have to goad him more. Then he sighed, tired and pained, and gritted: "Truth."

Honey considered. "What's your family like?"

He laughed scathingly. "Oh, *sure—*"

"Not in a *give us information on the enemy* way, dipshit," Honey said. "We just don't know anything about you." *Other than you're an uptight sophomore who insists on being called by his full name and isn't fun at parties,* she added privately, still smiling at him like he was hot shit.

He sighed. "My family's great. They'll be even better once I've proven myself."

"Proven yourself," Sadie repeated, shifting her tone from dubious to politely curious between the two words. She shot Honey a look, like: *how am I doing?*

Honey resisted the urge to give her a mocking thumbs up.

Alexander nodded, straightening out creases in his bedsheets in sharp, efficient movements. "I was supposed to lure you somewhere tonight and put you down."

"Bad job on all fronts," Honey said before she could stop herself.

"Obviously," he snarled. His arm muscles twitched. "It's...it's not the usual proving. Making sure vampires end up human. But however this week ends up, we'll have two less vampires. It will have to count."

"Wait," Sadie said slowly. "I thought you'd decided to go rogue. Your family sent you on this hunt? Alone? On purpose?"

He scowled at her. "It's a *proving*."

"You're sixteen," Sadie said. "You should be *proving yourself* by getting your license."

"Or getting laid," Honey added.

He huffed a loud, deeply fake laugh. His arms flexed again. If it was anyone else, it would've been hot. Alexander doing it made Honey think of dogs raising their hackles, puffing up their shoulders. Trying to look bigger when they were backed into a corner.

"Hope they don't miss Elijah too much," Honey said.

Sadie gave her a warning look. Honey ignored her, smiling harder at Alexander.

Alexander sniffed. "Elijah was a loner. None of us really knew him. When he emailed us about you, it was the first time we'd heard from him in years."

"Unlucky us," Sadie mumbled.

Alexander nodded. He looked over at Honey. "What about you? Truth or dare?"

Honey scoffed. "Nope. You didn't tell us anything about your family."

He looked unreasonably outraged. "I did!"

"*They're great* isn't an answer. Are your parents together? Any siblings?"

A strange look passed over his face. For a moment all the guarded mistrust fell away, and all that was left was a raw wound Honey didn't actually want to poke at.

Then the snarl came back, as sharp as ever. "Dare."

Honey looked over at Sadie, eyebrows raised in question.

Sadie rolled her eyes in reply. "Fine. Have you ever done the spring break yell?"

His snarl faltered. "The...?"

"SPRING BREEEEEEEAK," Honey and Sadie shrieked, so sudden and loud that Alexander's hand shot out toward the crossbow still lying on his bed.

"It's better if you yell it out of a car that's going full speed on a sunny day with fun music playing," Honey added, acting like she didn't notice his fingers tightening around the weapon.

"But wherever works," she continued. "Go on."

Alexander blinked. "It's past midnight."

"This is the cheapest motel in fifty miles. They're getting what they paid for." Honey leaned across Sadie to thump the wall, grinning when Sadie glared at her. "Go on! I dare you!"

"I..." Alexander gave them both an uncertain look, like the big kids were playing a joke on him in the playground. Then he steeled himself and yelped, "SPRING BREAK!"

Honey clapped. "That was pathetic! Louder!"

He glared, but a flimsy smile curled his lips. "SPRING BREEEEAK!"

Honey and Sadie threw their heads back. "SPRING BREEEEEEEAK," the three of them screamed as one.

Somebody banged on the motel wall. Honey giggled, digging her chin into Sadie's shoulder. Sadie shoved her playfully, no vampire strength. There was nothing fake about them grinning at each other.

Alexander watched them, still suspicious, but his mouth kept twitching. Then Honey heard it: the smallest laugh, almost lost under the girls' giggles.

We're getting there, Honey thought triumphantly.

chapter
eight

ALEXANDER ATE NEATLY, tucking small forkfuls of scrambled egg into his mouth and glaring at Sadie across the diner booth.

He stabbed a butter knife in her direction. "Don't touch my phone again."

"Totally," Sadie said.

They'd turned off his alarm. He'd woken up groggy and enraged after six hours of sleep, falling over himself as he searched for his socks and yelled about getting on the road. It had taken a lot of effort and some thinly veiled threats to calm him down enough to have breakfast at the diner across the road.

Make him like you, Honey had whispered before she left. Then, when Sadie gave her a desperate look: *Just keep him talking. He's bound to get attached.*

Attached. Like that stray cat Sadie's dad complained about for weeks and then started setting out food for.

"So," Sadie said. "Your family sounds fun."

He kept silent, slicing the corner off his toast with careful precision.

"Letting you go off on a hunt alone," Sadie continued. "They must trust you a lot."

"I can take care of myself." Alexander wiped a crumb off his lip, shooting a glance at the door. He'd insisted they sit there, and Sadie was only now realizing it was so he could see all the exits. His chair was up against the wall, so nobody could sneak up behind him. Just like in the restaurant.

"Your girlfriend's taking a long time to pick up supplies," he said.

"She's taking a normal amount of time, you're just paranoid." Sadie scratched her flannel shirt, still buttoned up over her bandages. Blood was seeping through the material, turning the plaid pattern black.

Just keep him talking, she reminded herself.

She swallowed. "Truth or dare?"

"No," he replied, loud enough that two other tables looked over. He smiled stiffly at them until they looked away, then leaned in to whisper, "*I'm* in charge. Truth or dare?"

It would've been funny if he didn't have his sports bag in his lap. His hands kept twitching around his utensils like he wanted to check the bag was still there, full of weapons that could kill her.

Sadie didn't have to think about it. There was no way she'd take a dare from this guy. "Truth."

He hesitated. The demanding energy from before

receded, like he hadn't actually come up with anything to say after telling her he was in charge.

"Uh," he said. "What are you going to do if it works? Killing your sire, turning human again?"

Sadie tried to think of an answer that would make him get attached to her. She couldn't think of any. Lying was exhausting, she'd done it so much—lying to her dad, to her teachers, to Honey—it made her want to curl up under the table and sleep. Even if she wasn't already tired from the arrow wound.

"Follow Honey to college," she answered. "Get some shitty job. Eventually get a less shitty job. I don't know. I can't think of anything I'd want for a career. I can't really...picture it. The rest of my life. Even before..."

She waved a hand at her mouth.

Alexander looked thoughtful and a little resentful. Of what, Sadie couldn't begin to guess. There was still the glimmer of suspicion on his face, but it was hard to see behind everything else going on.

"It's...admirable of you. You're very loyal to each other." He paused. Ate another neat forkful of eggs, considering.

Sadie itched absently at her shirt. Black fluid crept under her fingernails. She was still weak. She'd spent hours lying on that motel bed with Honey, and when she got up she'd almost fallen right back down. *I'm fine,* she'd said when Honey bolted back to her side, but it had taken Honey another full minute to let her go.

"Last year we tracked down this couple," Alexander said slowly. "A husband and wife. He turned her. And when we cornered the wife, he just...turned and fled. It was..." Alexander's fork scraped against his plate. He winced at the metallic screech, or maybe at his memories. His voice was low, mouth twisting as he continued, "It was *disgusting* how fast he abandoned her to save his own skin."

Sadie almost told him about Honey saving her life in that dingy bar bathroom. Honey's hands on her face as she bled out, Honey's black hand smearing over her lips, making her drink. The desperation in her eyes. The cops could've burst in right then and Honey would've stayed. She would've bit and clawed her way back to Sadie no matter what.

But she couldn't say that. Alexander couldn't know Honey was her sire, not the vampire they were chasing. Not until he was dead and Sadie was still a monster— nothing left to hide behind.

The diner door swung open. There was no peach deodorant in the air, but Sadie could tell it was Honey anyway. That quick, bouncy step. She could pick Honey's footsteps out of a crowd in grade school. Even in the years they weren't talking, Sadie would hear Honey walk down a hall behind her and she'd know. She'd never look back. But she'd know.

Honey flounced over to their booth, scooched in next to Sadie, and dropped a plastic bag at their feet. "You guys get the best part of truth and dare are the dares, right? You can't just keep saying truth. Sadie, you used to be better at this."

"Because you threaten me until I pick dare," Sadie pointed out.

Honey rolled her eyes. Her gaze lingered on Sadie's shirt, the black stain blotting Sadie's fingers.

Sadie wiped her hand on her jeans, took Honey's hand and squeezed. *I'm fine,* said the squeeze. Too late, she realized she hadn't gotten all the black slick off her hand, and Honey's pinkie was streaked with it. She tried to untangle her fingers, but Honey held fast.

"What's that?" Alexander asked.

For a moment Sadie thought he meant their joined hands. Then she saw the pamphlet Honey was holding in her Sadie-less hand.

"These," Honey announced, brandishing a pamphlet that looked like a rip-off of the Graphic Design Is My Passion meme, "are the tourist attractions I was telling you about."

"Oh," said Sadie, who had not been told. "Great."

Honey unfolded the pamphlet on the table, pointing to each attraction in turn. "America's largest collection of Dolly Parton memorabilia. World's largest taxidermied crocodile. Museum dedicated to a TV show that ended before we were born. Oooh, Sadie, there's a *cave—*"

"I'm not following anyone into a cave," Alexander said flatly.

"Boo," Honey replied. "Cross out Alexander."

She crossed the air in front of his face. Sadie joined

in, ignoring how Alexander's grip tightened on his utensils.

Honey sat back in her chair, sliding her arm over Sadie's shoulders. "And then the haunted theme park in Fester, obviously. We have to go to that before we find our sire."

"A haunted theme park," Alexander asked. "In spring?"

"Yearlong attraction, lil' bit." Honey slid the pamphlet over to him. Sadie wanted to take a look—she'd never heard of a haunted theme park—but she was too focused on Honey's arm over her shoulder. Easy, casual. No hidden glances from across a room, no meeting in the dark woods.

For a second Sadie let herself imagine the impossible: they killed the bassist and both turned human. Honey could go off to college. Sadie could follow without the potential of ruining both their lives with bloodshed. They could find a favorite food place off campus and sit there, Honey's arm over her shoulder, two regular girls who were hungry for normal things that didn't hurt anybody.

Numbness pulsed through Sadie's chest, making her flinch with surprise. Honey glanced over at her, gaze zeroing in on the black stain in Sadie's flannel shirt.

"I'm fine," Sadie assured her.

Honey smiled. It took a second too long.

chapter
nine

HALFWAY THROUGH AMERICA'S largest collection of Dolly Parton memorabilia, Alexander turned to Honey and said, "You're not taking this situation as seriously as you should."

"No idea what you're talking about," Honey replied. Then she reached up and slid a Dolly wig onto his head.

Alexander glared. He hunched his wide shoulders between the narrow shelves of Dolly memorabilia, ducking his head to avoid the low ceiling. The roadside attraction was actually a small house, and the builders hadn't considered that people over six feet existed.

It had been a weird two days. Alexander had done his best to remain Tough Guy Stoic, sitting in the passenger seat with his arms crossed and only participating in I Spy when Honey threatened him with unending renditions of "The Wheels On The Bus." Lecturing them on the importance of weapon care and then shutting up when he realized he shouldn't help the enemy. Pretending not to laugh at Sadie's incorrect but wildly funny answers on *Jeopardy*. He kept having these moments where Honey suspected he could be fun to be around if he only got away from his family's clutches long enough to relax. He wanted to, she was sure of it. He wanted to party and have fun and he *wanted* to like them. They just had to convince him it was worth going against everything he knew.

"I'm serious," Alexander said. "I..."

He stopped and ripped the wig off his head, scowling. His elbow caught on a row of ceramic Dolly lookalikes, swatting three of them off the shelf in one sweep.

"Shit." He lunged for them with his clumsy human reflexes.

Honey watched him, amused. Her hands flashed out, returning the ceramics back to the shelf in one smooth, swift motion.

"You were saying," she prompted.

He stared at the ceramics like he was going to thank her. Then he blinked, and the reluctant gratefulness was replaced by his usual arrogance. "This is your *life*. If you don't do this *right*, and *on time*, I'll have to..."

He shot a cautious look around the room. An elderly couple was examining a pristine T-shirt in a glass case on the mantel. In the next room, Sadie bumped her head on a low-hanging lamp and swore.

"Take care of it," he continued. "And I don't..."

He stopped. As he lifted his arms to fold tight over his large chest, his elbows side-swiped those same ceramics he'd just tipped over. They wobbled dangerously.

"Come *on*," he complained, holding his hand in front of them so they wouldn't fall. He kept looking at them after they stopped wobbling, and Honey listened to his teeth grind in his mouth.

She grinned. "Aw. You don't want to kill us."

He shushed her. The elderly couple across the room admired the T-shirt, oblivious.

"You *like* us," Honey cooed, making sure to keep it teasing and slightly sexy instead of deeply relieved. *Thank god,* she thought. *This might actually work.*

"That's not what I said," Alexander hissed. "I'm saying you need to take this *seriously*. Go straight to Fester. Not mess around at stupid roadside attractions that make you pay two dollars to go in a musty old house with ceilings that can only fit middle schoolers."

"These ceilings *suck*," Sadie called from the other room.

"I don't know what you guys are talking about," Honey said in all her five-two glory. "This place is awesome."

"Ha, ha." Sadie hunched toward them, bending to clear the doorway and venture into the shelves, coming to a stop behind Honey. It was too narrow to stand at her side. She looked at Honey pointedly. Now or never.

Honey nodded, turning back to Alexander. "Okay, now we're all bonded—"

"Not bonded," Alexander said.

She ignored him. "Sadie isn't healing. We ate *so* many animals on the drive yesterday, and we're thinking animals just won't cut it. You hearing me?"

Alexander went still. "I better not be," he said slowly. It would've been more threatening if he wasn't hunched to avoid a low ceiling.

"We need to be fueled up for the fight," Honey said. "Either you let us nip and quit some jackass off the street, or she feeds off of you."

She meant the last part as a joke. Mostly. Later, she would reason she was testing the waters, seeing if they were at that place yet. In the moment, it was just... instinct. Honey liked pushing people for a laugh. Old habits die hard.

Alexander's blue eyes went savage. His teeth clenched, his lip curling up as if Honey had suggested they go over and club the elderly couple to death with their own canes.

"I'd rather die than let you feed off me," he said, loud enough that the elderly couple looked over.

Honey waved at them. After a pointed nudge, Sadie did, too.

They nodded back awkwardly and shuffled out of the room.

"You're no fun," Honey told him. "Fine, no teeth in Alexander. You gotta let her snack on *someone*. She can't fight the sire with a hole in her chest. Sadie, show him your hole."

"I'm not showing him my..." Sadie's nose scrunched at the wording. "He can see the blood. He knows."

Alexander's gaze ticked down to the black stain over her chest. Honey had replaced the bandage an hour ago and it had already bled through. He looked at her limp hair, the bags under her eyes.

"She's *weak*," Honey tried. "We can't fight him like this. We'll pick some creep, okay? *You* can pick him. Some real jerk—"

"No," Alexander snapped. "I'm not letting you hurt anybody. I'm a hunter, I protect people from things like you."

Honey rolled her eyes. "Oh my god—"

"This discussion is over." Alexander tried to storm off, hindered by the narrow shelves and his wide limbs. He knocked over a Dolly mug and a Dolly saltshaker on his way out of the room, only stopping to shove the broken pieces under the shelves.

"It's fine," Sadie said once he was gone. "We'll just... eat more before North Carolina."

She smiled, strained. Honey tried to remember the last time she'd seen Sadie look rested, *properly* rested, sated and whole. All through high school Honey had snuck glances over at Sadie and found her sallow and exhausted and pale. This last year only made it worse. Feeding didn't cure it. While Honey got flushed cheeks and shiny hair, Sadie's eyebags got less dark and her skin went from translucent to printer paper white.

Honey took her hand, turning around carefully so as not to jostle the endless Dolly memorabilia.

"We'll sneak away at the haunted theme park tonight," she told Sadie. "Get you someone to eat. I get not wanting to get chomped on, but he's being *super* irrational about this."

"*So* irrational," Sadie echoed, only half-mocking, like she was trying to talk herself into it. "How are we sneaking away? He's watching us like a hawk."

She tensed. Honey cocked her head and listened to Alexander argue with the guy out front that he didn't have to pay another two dollars, he was already just *in* there, and he needed to get back in to check on something *very* important.

"We'll figure it out," Honey said.

Later, her shirt drenched in raccoon blood, Honey called her mom.

"I see my daughter finally decided to call," Bree Williams said sourly. She was still mad at Honey for skipping the last day of school before spring break.

Honey sighed. If her mom wasn't going to bother with pleasantries, she wasn't either. "What if I don't go to college?"

"Why wouldn't you?" Bree asked slowly, threat and worry blending, like she was deciding if she needed to yell or not. "College was always the plan. And you got so many *scholarships*."

"I know." Honey winced, holding the phone away from her slick chin. She'd gotten blood on the bottom of the phone case.

"And you love school!"

"I know," Honey repeated. "I just...somebody needs to take care of Sadie."

A disappointed silence took over. Honey closed her eyes, straining to hear if anybody was in danger of stumbling on a bloody girl in the middle of the woods. No one close enough to worry about. Still, she wanted an excuse to end this call. It was hard enough making herself dial the number, let alone keep this conversation going. Part of her would love to scream "LOL, PSYCH" and hang up to her mom yelling at her.

"I know she's your person," Bree said. "But you can't let one person derail your life. Did she *ask* you to take care of her?"

"Ugh. No. She'd cuss me out if she knew about this." Honey drew a heart in the dirt with her shoe. A drop of blood landed in the middle of it.

"Sometimes you can't help people out of a hole," Bree said, in that strained tone that meant she was trying to remember quote posts she'd seen on Facebook. "You can just...sit there with them. I don't know, is that helpful?"

"No, mom, you suck." Something shifted in the bushes fifty feet away. Honey's head snapped around. "I gotta go. I have to rip out a deer's throat and bleed it into a Hello Kitty thermos."

Bree sighed. "I don't understand you kids and your memes."

"It's all over TikTok, mom. Bye." Honey hung up, tucked the thermos in her elbow, and started stalking.

There was still some tasty, tasty blood under her fingernails when she got back to the motel. Honey sucked at it, the thermos dangling from her hand.

She was reaching for the doorknob when she heard it: hushed whispers from around the corner.

Honey took her finger out of her mouth and listened. It was definitely Alexander, she recognized that stupid snobby voice.

"No, mom," Alexander said. "I got it. I wrote it on the map and everything."

A woman's voice came through the other end: *"You didn't memorize it?"*

"I'm *going* to memorize it, I just need to—"

"You really should be able to memorize things by now."

"No, I know."

"We went through a lot of trouble getting this address for you."

Honey's hand tightened around the thermos. Address? Did his family track down Honey's sire?

"I got it, Mom." Alexander's voice softened. "I won't let you down."

"I know you won't."

Footsteps. Honey busied herself with the doorknob.

"I'll be home before school starts," he said as he rounded the corner. "Bye, Mom."

He saw Honey and froze.

Honey waved the thermos. "Aw, are you talking to your Mommy? Tell her I say hi!"

"No," Alexander said, and ended the call. He nodded down at the pink thermos. "That was fast."

"I'm a very efficient hunter." Honey flashed her fangs, grinning when Alexander gave the empty parking lot a nervous look.

Honey stood there, waiting. Was he going to tell her where her sire was? Or did he have something bigger planned?

"So?" She prompted.

"So what?" Alexander said, glaring. He was annoyed, but more than that he was scared. Scared she *knew*.

Honey gestured at the phone in his hand. "How was dear old Mom?"

"Fine," Alexander said, voice clipped.

Honey turned back to the door. She wasn't disappointed, she told herself as she let them into the musty motel room. Just because they'd had a few good moments together didn't mean he was a good guy. Didn't mean they could *trust* him. He was a hunter. He was raised in it. They weren't going to undo that in one spring break, no matter how many tourist traps they dragged him to.

chapter
ten

SADIE HAD BEEN HOLDING her breath since she walked into Fester's one and only theme park. It didn't help. The scents rose in overwhelming waves of sweat and cotton candy and sweet, sweet blood rushing under everyone's flimsy skin.

"I didn't know they made black cotton candy," Honey announced as they looked out over the evening crowd of theme park-goers. "Another thing on my TBE list."

Alexander lowered his free bat mask. "TBE?"

"To Be Eaten," Honey explained, shooting Sadie a grin. It faded once she saw Sadie's face.

Sadie tried to rearrange her expression into something that wasn't exhausted and hungry, but it was too late. Honey gave her the pointed eyebrows that meant: *Go Time.*

"Hey Alex," Honey said. "Truth or dare?"

"*Alexander*," Alexander corrected. He shook his head

in disapproval. "I can't believe we're in Fester and we're *here* instead of chasing down your sire."

He looked out over the park, like he was cataloging exit strategies. They could see every spiky fence from the park entrance. It was smaller than it looked on the pamphlet—the main attraction was the haunted house, everything else had been built around it. Food carts and fortune tellers and a puny Ferris wheel with plastic spiderwebs glued between the spokes. They didn't even have a roller coaster. Honey told them in the van on the way over—it had closed in 2011 after it derailed and crashed into the carousel. Fourteen injuries, one of which ended in an amputation. No deaths.

"Aleeeex," Honey goaded. "Truth! Or! Dare!"

Alexander gave the park one last scrutinizing look and turned back to Honey. "Dare."

Honey beamed at Sadie. "You heard him. Give him a dare."

If Sadie could sweat, she would be dripping.

"Uh," she said. "Dare you...to let us fly you somewhere."

He got that same outraged look he'd had in the Dolly Parton house, like letting them touch him with their vampire powers would disgrace his hunter soul.

"Come onnn," Honey goaded. "Gotta use it before we lose it! And it's not like we can *fly*-fly, it's more of a hover. Quit freaking out."

"I'm not freaking out," Alexander said, too fast. "I just...people will see."

"This coming from the guy who shot us in a restaurant," Honey said flatly. "It's all part of the show. Sadie—go."

Sadie wrapped her arms around Alexander's surprisingly narrow waist and lifted him off the ground. Alexander squawked, grabbing her elbows.

"Alex," Sadie said. "Are you afraid of heights?"

"I can't afford to be afraid of anything," Alexander said, his voice high and strange as they cleared the first floor of the haunted house. People pointed and gasped. A child twirled on the ground, yelling at Sadie to pick her next.

"Wave," Sadie told him.

Alexander scowled at her. Then he waved, grudging and stiff. The twirling child giggled, and his wave loosened. Then he looked at the ground again and the color leached out of his face. He dropped his hand back to grip Sadie's arms like a climber grabbing a safety harness.

"This is high enough," he snapped.

"Not yet," Sadie told him, straining. They were two stories up, almost at the roof. She'd never flown this high before. It ached, like stretching a muscle too hard. Her whole body pulsed with strange pain as she floated them onto the roof.

"Ow," she said, stumbling onto the tiles. For a moment she worried about putting all her weight on the shabby roof. Then she saw the mold was painted on, the spiderwebs were cotton, the holes were too perfect to be born from neglect or storm damage. They'd be fine up here. Alexander would, anyway.

He peered cautiously over the edge. "This is so stupid," he said with a jittery laugh. It was almost sweet. Like they were just a bunch of teenagers playing dumb party games, and none of them had thought about murdering each other all week.

He looked over at her. "Uh, truth or dare?"

"Let's put a pin in that," Sadie said, and stepped off the roof.

Alexander's nervous smile guttered. "What?"

"I need to eat," Sadie said as she floated down slowly. "I won't kill anyone! It'll just be a bad memory, the worst they'll get is, like, *minor* PTSD." She paused at the first floor. "Other than this, you're having fun, right? A little?"

"I will *end* you," he hissed.

"Cool," Sadie called up at him. "Ten minutes."

Honey led her into the darkest part of the haunted house: a hallway lined with curtains, and automatons jumping out and shrieking at random intervals.

"Okay," Sadie said as they hunched beside a steel cutout of a witch. "Who are we picking? It's not going to be nice for them, I still can't do venom. Even *with* the venom it's still kinda like dosing someone."

"We're vampires, babe. We gotta get a little hazy with our morals." Honey pulled the heavy curtain back. "Pick anyone. Next person to come through that door."

A pair of twelve-year-old girls in matching unicorn shirts crept through the door, arms linked.

"Ew," Honey said. "Pick the *next* person to come through that door."

A teenage girl came through, picking her nails and looking bored. She had a septum piercing just like Sadie and looked deeply bored. She smelled like cigarette smoke, her heartbeat steady under the thin skin of her throat.

Sadie's mouth filled with saliva.

"Try not to pee your pants," the girl called to the young pair tugging each other down the hall and into the next room. A big sister, Sadie figured in the small part of her brain that wasn't screaming for blood.

"I'll give her venom," Honey said.

Sadie didn't have time to ask what she meant before Honey shot out, dragging the girl into the curtains.

The girl's heartbeat picked up, breath catching. "Whoa, hey, this is *way*—"

"Shhh," Honey said, her eyes turning black. "You're fine."

She sunk her teeth into her neck.

The girl's yelp trailed off into a moan. Her stiff limbs turned loose and liquid, her head lolling sideways to give Honey better access. Blood rolled toward her collarbone. Sadie leaned in to lick it up before digging her teeth in, right under Honey's bite.

It was like an atomic bomb going off in Sadie's veins, electric and vibrant and everything she'd ever wanted. It lit her synapses on fire, made her press closer and bite harder.

The girl moaned again, pain laced with pleasure. Honey's fangs sank deeper, sending another burst of venom through her system, and the pained moan faded into a pleased sigh. Later, Sadie would be grateful. But in that moment all she cared about was the blood. She drank and drank, each pull a fresh burst of ecstasy.

Honey's hand tangled in her hair, tugging. She detached herself from the girl's neck.

"Okay," she rasped. "Time to stop."

Sadie growled, biting harder. The girl whimpered. The venom was draining away.

Honey's eyes flickered, brown seeping through. "I *said—*"

The curtains ripped back. Large hands wrapped around her shoulders, dragging her back. Sadie resisted, hugging the girl close so she didn't have to stop biting.

"Hey," Honey snapped. "I'm handling it!"

"Like HELL," Alexander screamed. He started saying something else, but it got cut off with a grunt. Honey had kicked him.

"I got it," Honey said. "Hey, I said I *got* it. Sadie? Babe? Cut it out."

A hand wrapped around Sadie's neck. She growled, trying to buck it off. The hand stayed there, unrelenting.

Honey's mouth pressed against her ear. "*Stop*," she

commanded. "Or I'll let him stab you. Somewhere unimportant."

Sadie whined. It vibrated wetly against the girl's neck, which was lax under her mouth. The girl wasn't moaning anymore, her heartbeat weak, her body limp in Sadie's arms.

"I'll let him stab you in the leg," Honey warned. "Want a leg stab? No? Then let her go."

Sadie let her jaw relax. Just a little.

Honey ripped her head back. Sadie growled, but Honey was too fast, shoving the girl out of Sadie's arms. Sadie tried to dive for her, but Honey held her fast, arms tight around her squirming, skinny frame.

"Give her a second," she barked at Alexander, who had a knife in each hand, crouched and ready to stab.

Sadie snarled. She sucked desperately at her lips, cleaning the blood that was left there. Then it was gone, and her head started to clear. It was like swimming through mud. Sadie shuddered, held herself still.

"There we go," Honey whispered. She let Sadie go, eyeing her carefully. "That's my girl. Do you—Hey!"

Alexander grabbed Sadie and slammed her into the wall, both knives at her throat. Sadie hissed as they burned lines into her skin.

"I have to be strong," Sadie gasped, trying to remember the words. Part of her was still clawing herself out of the hunger. "To kill the sire. She's not dead, you can check—"

Alexander didn't even look at the girl bleeding on the

carpet. His eyes were wide and shiny with betrayal, mouth twisted in disgust.

"We're cool," Sadie tried. "Okay? We're cool. We can finish that game of truth or dare, I'm sorry I had to trick you."

"Don't try and *bond* with me," he snarled. "I'm such an idiot. I know—I *know* what you are. You're a soulless, bloodthirsty monster. Nothing else."

"We're going to kill our sire," Sadie croaked. "We're gonna be human—"

"Just a few more days," Honey said behind them, tense and ready to launch herself at him any second. "We'll be human by the end of spring break. We didn't lie."

A laugh jolted out of Sadie's trapped throat. They were lying. By the end of the week Honey *might* be human, but Sadie was still doomed to a crappy life, sneaking around dingy motels and trying not to be a serial killer.

Alexander's chest heaved. His cheeks were flushed. Sadie told herself it didn't make her hungry.

"Shit," Alexander spat. He let Sadie go and staggered back. For a moment he just stood there, eyes wide and wet. He'd never looked younger, his hands shaking around the knives he'd just had at Sadie's throat.

He turned around.

Sadie panicked. If he left, they had no idea where their sire was.

She moved forward. But before Sadie could grab him, Honey shoved him up against the wall.

"Can't leave," she told him. "Not without telling us where our sire is."

He glared at her.

"We know you know," Sadie said. "Your mom gave you an address."

"That wasn't—" Alexander's lips thinned. "It's back at the motel. Now let *go* of me, or I will run you through."

Honey let him go. Alexander brushed his shirt down like she'd tainted him with her filth. Then he stormed out of the hallway.

Honey wiped her mouth clean, smearing blood over the back of her hand. "They don't teach hunters how to hotwire vans, right?"

She gave Sadie a hesitant smile. She was trying so *hard*, and it was breaking Sadie's heart.

"For the love of god," Sadie told her. "Whatever you're hiding, just *say* it. Do you not want to be with me anymore? Because I'd understand! Stop dangling this shit over my head and let it fall already!"

Honey stared. She looked...hurt. Sadie hadn't seen her so openly hurt since they were kids and Sadie smacked her pinkie away, ending their friendship for most of high school.

"I'm not *breaking up with you*," she said, like that was the stupidest thing Sadie had ever said. Like there wasn't an unconscious body right next to them who Sadie had nearly killed because she couldn't control her own hunger.

Honey sighed. "I never accepted the Berkeley offer, okay?"

Sadie stared at her, waiting for her to do jazz hands and yell "psych!" It didn't come.

"The acceptance deadline's in, like...a *week*," Sadie said, dazed. "Your mom keeps sending me articles about crime rates in California! And job listings for unqualified losers!"

"I can't go to college like this!" Honey's hands halted mid-gesture, but Sadie knew: she'd been about to wave down at Sadie with blood over her chin, shaking and monstrous. "We need to be able to pack up and run at a moment's notice. I can't do that at college."

"But...you want to discover new bugs!"

"I'll find a way," Honey said. "Jesus, stop over-reacting."

"*I'm* overreacting?" Sadie barked a desperate laugh. "You love school! If student loans weren't a thing you'd do school until you were forty. You're *going* to college. You're getting friends you actually like. You're getting a LIFE—"

"And you'd hate it," Honey spat. "If I'm at college, or if we're running around the country, you're stuck working some job you hate, keeping your life shitty and small, and trying not to kill everybody you walk past. You'd *hate* it. You *need* to be human again."

Honey set her jaw like she wanted to be bitchy, but

the worry seeped through, thick and cloying. Sadie hated it.

"I've kept my life shitty and small for a while," Sadie said slowly. "And even back before all this crap, I was... hungry. I was *so* hungry all the time. If I got turned human right now, I'd be drinking."

Honey groaned. "Sadie—"

"Don't." Sadie shoved a finger in her face. "*Don't* tell me I'm overreacting. You saved my life with that road trip last year, and I was *still* drinking. It was...it was *in* me. The hunger. First time I drank, it was that same feeling. Maybe I didn't go feral and start biting people, but I didn't...I couldn't stop. Even if life got *good*, I couldn't stop."

"You don't know that," Honey said quietly.

"Trust me. I know." Sadie let out another laugh. It cracked around the edges. "Maybe I'm just meant for a small, shitty life, Hon. Human or vampire. Ever think of that?"

The hallway was silent. A tinny cackle came over the speakers, the static making both of them wince.

The door slid open at the end of the hall. The two kids from before crept in, arguing quietly. They saw their sister's body on the floor and stopped.

"Um," said the taller one, pointing. "Is that Rachel?"

"She passed out," Honey told them. "You should call an ambulance. Do you have a phone?"

"*Do I have a phone,*" said the taller one mockingly,

pulling out a phone that looked like it cost more than Sadie's van. "Did she hit her head?"

Before either of them could answer, a steel automaton of a witch slammed out of the wall. A piercing screech played over the speakers, making everyone jolt.

Everybody except Sadie, who turned to the witch automaton and screamed back, fangs thickening in her mouth, eyes flooding black. It was so loud and so high-pitched the taller kid dropped her phone in her haste to grab her ears.

The witch was rosy-cheeked and hook-nosed, its mouth stuck in a menacing grin. Sadie punched it. It snapped off its hinges. Sadie didn't stick around to watch it settle on the bloody carpet before she turned and ran, ignoring Honey's yells as the hallway door swung shut.

chapter
eleven

HONEY FOUND her in the motel bathtub. Clothes on, faucet running, stripped down to her bra and bandages. For a moment Honey just stood there, overcome with relief. She never thought Sadie would run off for good. But she could always do something stupid.

Honey held up the car keys. "Thanks for leaving these in Steve-van."

"Thank Alexander for not hotwiring it and driving off." Sadie lifted her head. "Is he around?"

"Do you hear his weirdly quiet footsteps? Smell his fancy deodorant?"

Sadie shook her head.

"Then no." Honey got on her knees next to the bathtub. *How the tables turn*, she wanted to say. They'd done exactly this last year, Honey in the bathtub and Sadie perched next to her. What had she told Honey as she offered up her scraped palms? *Behave*. And Honey had, keeping her fangs tucked away as she licked Sadie's palms clean.

Sadie's hand hung over the side. Honey reached for it. Before she could touch her cool skin, Sadie pulled it away, curling her hands over her chest.

They'd switched, Honey thought sadly. Now it was Honey taking care of Sadie, and Sadie was way too sad to make it fun.

Honey asked, "Is it healing?"

"A little." Sadie grudgingly moved her hands down. The black hole above her bra was smaller than in the morning. Less gory.

"No leak," Honey said approvingly. "You won't soak the bandage through this time."

Sadie grunted. Her head lolled back, staring at the water-stained ceiling. "So much for the *endearing me to Alexander* plan."

"What do you mean? That went great. He didn't even stab us." Honey reached over and tweaked Sadie's hair, hoping for a giggle. Sadie didn't look at her. Honey felt the old urge to turn her hurt back on Sadie, tell Sadie to suck it up and quit being a loser. But the past year of looking over her shoulder and sneaking around and trying to cheer Sadie up had changed her, and the urge went away quickly.

"Does he really think we don't have *souls*?" she said. "What is this, *Buffy*?"

Sadie held up a piece of paper folded to the size of an eraser. Honey took it.

"It was the only thing he left in the room," Sadie said.

Honey unfolded it. It was a map of Fester, ripped from a pamphlet. There was an X scribbled on in red marker on the edge of town, near the woods.

Honey swallowed. He'd sounded so shady on the phone to his mom. And there had been a moment back at the fair where he'd snarled, *that isn't*—what was he about to say? Was he leading them into a trap? Some hunter's den ready to slaughter them both?

Then again, what else did they have to go on?

"Could be a parting gift," Honey said. "Maybe he feels shitty for abandoning us."

"Yeah," Sadie said dully. "Maybe." She turned off the faucet and heaved herself up. Clear water sluiced down her legs.

Honey tore her gaze away from Sadie's slim thighs. "Wait, we're going *now*?"

"Why not?"

Honey didn't bother bringing up Sadie's still-healing chest. Or Alexander, who could pop back up any moment with a crossbow. Or how they just had a screaming argument they should probably talk about before doing yet another thing that would put them through the emotional wringer.

"Dibs driving," she said instead.

The house was nice. *Too* nice.

"Are we sure this is it?" Honey whispered as they crept up to the fence.

Sadie frowned down at the map. "It's the only house around."

"I was imagining a shitty motel," Honey said. She peered up at the two-story house through the dark. It looked...*sweet*. Cozy. It had a wraparound porch with columns to prop it up. Hydrangea bushes clustered the yard. It had *trellises*. It looked like—

"Holy shit."

Sadie jerked. "What?"

Honey pointed through the fence. "It's an almost exact replica of the *Gilmore Girls* house!"

Sadie stared. Her eyes widened in awe. "Oh, shit."

"Right? If the paint job was different, and the bushes weren't there. And the windows were...I don't know. Longer? It's totally the same."

"Huh," Sadie said quietly. Something soft crossed her face. Honey had the strange sensation that she was watching all of Sadie unfold at once: Sadie at five years old, crying over a bee sting. Sadie at eight, cutting Honey's hair with craft scissors. Sadie at twelve, sobbing in Honey's arms the night her mom left. Sadie at sixteen, pretending not to see Honey in the hall. Sadie at eighteen, dripping blood and snarling.

Sadie smoothed out the map. "Maybe we're reading it wrong. We can—"

Honey cut her off. "This idea that you're doomed to

some small, shitty life is the biggest bullshit I've ever heard."

"*Okay*," Sadie muttered. She worried at the map, her thumb digging a hole through the town limits. She didn't look at Honey as she said, "It's not bullshit. I've known for years—"

"Oh my GOD," Honey said, loud enough that Sadie shushed her. Honey ignored it. The past year had changed her, but she was still Honey Williams. Making fun of people was hardwired in.

"You're eighteen, and you know exactly how your life is going to turn out!"

"Honey—"

"Of course you're right, what was I *thinking*? You just get this gut feeling when you're a teenager and everything unfolds exactly how you imagine it. *So* sorry I forgot about Basic Life Rules, *obviously* you're doomed forever—"

"*Honey*," Sadie snapped, voice dark and urgent as she stared over Honey's shoulder. She lunged, but it was too late.

Honey turned. A knife blurred past her cheek. Two seconds earlier and it would have gone through her skull.

"Not hot," Honey squeaked.

The knife bounced off the sidewalk. The curved blade was strangely familiar.

"Shit," said a voice from the trees.

Honey looked up. The last member of The Bleeding Bastards stood just beyond the tree line, as tall and gangly as ever. His hair was streaked with dirt. Dried blood flecked under his fingernails. He was wearing, of all things, an orange poncho. It didn't suit him.

The bassist held up another knife. It had a diamond carved neatly into the handle.

"Alex," Honey whispered. "That little—"

The bassist whipped the knife at them. Honey thanked all her vampire reflexes as they both leapt out of the way, the knife narrowly missing Sadie's shin.

"Van," Honey blurted. The blessed guitar was still in the backseat. One strum of that bad boy and her sire would fall to his knees. She made it one step before a knife bounced off the asphalt next to her shoes.

"He said it was you or me," the bassist yelled. "Guess who I pick?"

He sprinted at them, knives raised.

Honey scanned for the knives on the sidewalk. One had rolled into the deserted road, not far away. Honey bent down, but the bassist was too fast. He'd be on her in seconds—

The bassist grunted as Sadie barreled into him, knocking him to the ground.

"VAN," Sadie screamed.

Honey grabbed the knife off the road and stood. Steve-van was parked around the corner, because they were idiots who didn't want to tip off anyone in the house by parking out front.

I refuse to die in front of Lorelai Gilmore's house, Honey thought as she ran. *I refuse to die, period.*

Sadie screamed. Honey spun back, her mind empty of anything but the agony in her girlfriend's shout.

A silver arrow stuck out of Sadie's shoulder. She stumbled back from the bassist, who was looking around the trees looking equally excited and shocked.

A voice, smooth and smarmy, echoed down the street.

"Let's finish this," said Alexander White, and held up his crossbow.

chapter
twelve

SADIE FLUNG herself out of the way. The next arrow sunk into the bassist's leg, and he roared in pain.

"Get it," Sadie choked, clutching her injured shoulder. The silver burned around her fingers.

Alexander readied his crossbow again. He had a torch strapped to his head. It looked deeply stupid, but there were no streetlights around. *Needs must*, Sadie thought, her skin crawling as Alexander reached for the trigger.

Honey ran into the road between them, trying for casual and failing terribly. "What's the plan, huh? Corral us into one place and pick us off one by one?"

"Plus the vamp who lives there." Alexander jerked his head toward the house he'd marked on the map. His hands trembled around his crossbow, but his blue eyes were determined. "Go on the hunt for two, end up killing four. The best proving since Granddad."

"Mommy and Daddy will be so proud," Honey

crooned. She was stalling, Sadie realized. Which meant Sadie had to do...something.

Sadie turned back to the bassist and shoved him as hard as she could. He slammed through the fence and landed in the yard, broken panels of wood littered around him. He had run from the bathroom, Sadie remembered. The love of his life and his fiercest friends were in trouble and he'd fled the scene.

Sadie gripped the arrow in her shoulder. Her fingers burned. *Don't think about the pain,* she told herself. She ripped the arrow out, screaming through her teeth.

The bassist sat up with a groan. She shoved him back down, plunging the arrow through his hand and trapping his arm in the grass.

"Help us kill him," Honey said from the street as the bassist bellowed. "We can be human again—"

"That's not my problem! My job is killing vampires. I should've killed you days ago."

Footsteps on asphalt. Sadie looked up to see Alexander charging at them, Honey blurring around the corner toward the van.

The bassist reached for the arrow in his hand, whimpering. Sadie wrenched the arrow out of his leg and lunged. The arrow stabbed through his wrist and into the ground.

He howled.

Sadie stood, her hands scored with burns. Alexander surged through the gate, crossbow up.

"Wait for Honey to get back," Sadie told him.

Alexander shot a bolt through the bassist's right shin, then his left. The bassist cried and writhed, pinned to the ground like a butterfly.

Alexander advanced on him, unsheathing the ax from his belt. It glinted cruelly in the moonlight, the edge deadly sharp.

"It *has* to be Honey," Sadie told him.

Alexander still didn't look at her.

"Please," the bassist begged. "I'll give you anything."

"Give me death," Alexander said, voice shaking. He raised the ax over his head.

Sadie stormed in front of him, grabbing the ax handle. The stench of burned flesh filled the air, Sadie's eyes filling with black tears as the burn went deep.

"It has to be Honey," she growled wetly.

"Why? You're the feral one. If anything, you..." Alexander's eyes narrowed. "You're not his."

A black tear dripped down Sadie's cheek. The heat got worse every second; her fingers burned black around the ax handle.

"No," she whispered. "I'm Honey's."

She watched the realization dawn over his face: she'd never kill Honey. She was stuck like this.

"So...I would've had to kill you anyway."

Sadie shook her head. "You don't *have* to do anything."

"This is what I was born for." He yanked on the ax. Bits of charred flesh flecked onto his sleeves, and he winced. "Getting rid of monsters."

"We're not monsters." Sadie gritted her teeth, shaking with the effort of holding the ax at bay. "We're *teenagers*. Just let Honey—"

A pair of hands locked around her ankles and yanked. Sadie fell back with the bassist's arms locked around her neck. His hands were free, the arrows dripping black. He'd pulled them all the way up the silver column, up and off, and now he was wrenching at Sadie's chin, trying to bite her throat out.

Sadie punched at him, trying to turn around. He held her fast. Black blood smeared over her chin, his teeth grazing her shoulder as she bucked.

Alexander raised his ax even higher. He was a good shot, but he wasn't *that* good. Sadie and the bassist were moving too much for him to get a clear hit. If he brought it down on him, it would go through Sadie first.

The bassist's hand strayed too close to Sadie's mouth. Sadie latched on, biting a chunk out of his thumb, her gaze stuck on the ax hovering over them both.

Hesitating, she realized. *He really did get attached.*

The ax came down. The bassist screamed. The hand around Sadie's chin fell away, hanging by a few stubborn cords of sinew and skin. Alexander had cut most of the way through the bassist's wrist.

Sadie spat out the chunk of thumb and rolled off.

Alexander raised his ax again.

"Wait," Sadie blurted. "Just—"

A chaotic guitar note rang through the night. Then

another, then a frenzied cluster of notes played by someone who didn't know what they were doing.

"WE ARE *HONEYBLOODS*," Honey screamed as she tore around the corner. "HERE TO FUCK YOU UP!"

The bassist curled into himself, shoving his good hand against one ear and shrieking.

"It's the guitar," Sadie told a confused Alexander. "We blessed it with our bond."

Honey ran at them, strumming hard and fast. She looked relieved and a little disgusted to see the bassist curled up on the ground, bleeding from multiple holes and a cut-off hand.

Sadie held out a hand. Honey shot a worried look at her charred fingers, but passed the guitar over. Sadie settled her blackened hands over the strings, wincing through the pain. The messy guitar music turned into a song they'd only played once, the night Honey turned her. *Washing up in another motel bathroom...scrub that stain right outta your mouth...*

Honey turned to Alexander, "Give me the ax."

Alexander looked up. His gaze had been stuck on the symbol Milly had carved into the guitar, his expression unreadable.

"She's right here," Honey tried. "Quit being a dick and—"

Alexander held out the ax.

Honey hesitated. She pulled her sleeves down and

gripped the handle, wincing when her fingertips slipped past the fabric and started to burn.

"It was your diary, right?" she asked the bassist. "Your little black notebook, with the pining emo lyrics? Do you think he loved you back? 'Cause I kinda don't.'"

The bassist screamed up at her, fangs bared.

"You shouldn't have killed me," Honey whispered, and brought the ax down hard.

Black blood spurted down the bassist's poncho. His head rolled in the sticky grass.

Sadie's hands stilled on the guitar. The night was silent.

Honey tossed the ax away and straightened up, tense and waiting. "Did it work? Is it happening?"

"It won't happen straight away," Sadie said, mostly for Alexander's benefit. She didn't want him to grab the ax back just because Honey didn't get a heartbeat in the first ten seconds post-sire murder. She didn't actually know how long the de-vampirism process worked.

Honey stared down at the bassist's head. Her lower lip trembled.

"Hey," Sadie coaxed. She stepped over the bassist's skewered legs so she could take Honey's head in her hands, ignoring how her burned skin flecked off onto Honey's cheeks. "You did it. Everything's going to be fine."

"Totally," Honey said weakly. Her eyelids fluttered. "Sadie...I..."

Her eyes rolled up. Her knees folded, and she slumped into Sadie.

Sadie dropped the guitar to catch her, lowering her carefully to the ground. Alexander had to step back to make room for her head.

Sadie brushed hair out Honey's face, lovely even dotted with black blood. Same soft freckled cheeks. Same gap between her front teeth; same pouty mouth suited for mockery and mischief. Her skin was cool. Sadie curved a ruined palm down her jaw, waiting for warmth.

Alexander walked off, suspiciously silent. Sadie looked up to see Alexander crouching to pick up the ax from the front porch, where Honey had thrown it. He wiped off the black goo with his sleeve, a practiced motion that made Sadie's skin crawl.

She curled protectively around Honey. "Don't."

Alexander paused. He gave the ax another wipe, slower this time, lingering on the sharp tip. "Powerful bond. To bring that vampire to his knees like that"

Sadie blinked. "What?"

He pointed at the guitar. "You have something special," he told her. His throat worked, knuckles white from how hard he was clenching the ax. Standing above her on the porch, ax in hand, no moonlight touching him, Sadie forgot how young he was. He wasn't a sixteen-year-old kid anymore. He was just dangerous.

Then he swallowed, ducking his head, and he was a kid again. "Don't come home."

"But—"

He tucked the ax back into his holster. "I'll call them, tell them Honey's human. Once they confirm it, they'll leave her alone. But they'll find out about you. And once they know I let you go, they'll find me."

"Find you," Sadie repeated. "Where are you going?"

She pulled Honey further into her lap, pressing a thumb against her pulse point. It was useless—the numbness was setting in. She wouldn't be able to feel Honey's heartbeat in either of her burned hands.

Alexander shrugged bitterly. "I don't know. I...I failed my proving."

"Alexander," Sadie said. She didn't know what she would've said after that. *It will be okay? We'll protect you?* The kid had burned his life down for two girls he barely knew. What could she possibly say to that?

She didn't have to find out. A *click* from the side of the house made them both startle.

A middle-aged woman waved from further down the porch. She had fangs and a dressing gown and pink oven mitts. A silver crossbow dangled casually at her hip.

"Howdy," she said. "Someone mind explaining the dead vampire in my front yard?"

chapter
thirteen

HONEY WILLIAMS WOKE UP ALIVE.

Heartbeat and everything. She could feel it pounding away in her chest. Sadie's beloved face swam above her, pale and wondrous in the dark. Her charred fingers stroked a line down Honey's jaw.

"I can hear your heart," Sadie whispered.

Honey smiled and raised a hand to touch Sadie's face. Her fingers were burn-free. Nothing hurt.

Other voices crept into focus. Alexander was arguing with someone on the porch in front of them.

Honey sat up. Her head swam.

"Whoa." Sadie steadied her before she could fall back into her lap. "How do you feel?"

"Super sexy," Honey mumbled. She smacked her sluggish lips and pushed herself up again, grimacing at the decapitated corpse lying beside them. "Ew."

Alexander stood stiffly on the porch steps, clutching his ax holster. "I *said* I'm fine."

"Sure," said a middle-aged woman further down the porch. "You look *grand*, kid."

She readjusted something against her hip. Honey had to squint to make out the silver crossbow at her side, held in a pink oven mitt. It would've been easier if Alexander's head torch was aimed at it, but he kept it pointed at the woman's lightly lined face.

"Why don't you come in?" the woman said, an easy smile curving her full lips. She looked exceedingly calm for someone holding a deadly weapon. "We can get y'all cleaned up. I'm Rosaline. What's your name?"

"Don't touch me," Alexander snarled.

Honey tensed, waiting to see if this would turn into another fight. Alexander's knuckles were white and trembling around his holster. He glanced down at Honey and Sadie, sprawled in the grass among all that black blood.

"She's human," Sadie said hastily. "You can check."

Honey held out her wrist.

For a moment Alexander just stood there, torn between Rosaline and the girls he'd been trapped on a road trip with. Then he stomped down the porch steps and took Honey's wrist, pressing down hard on the pulse point.

"Huh," he said thinly. He jerked back, hand whipping back to his side. "Good. That's...good."

"Congratulations," called Rosaline from the porch. "I assume this was what you wanted?"

"Yeah," Honey said. She twisted to look at Sadie, still pale and dead. "Pretty much."

Sadie's mouth twitched in a sad smile. She knew what Honey was thinking. She didn't want Honey to feel sorry for her. Honey made a face—*get over yourself*—and Sadie snorted.

Alexander strode past them.

Sadie watched him break into a jog just before the gate. "Is he just—"

"He's fully leaving," Honey said, and raised her voice. "Don't steal Steve-van!"

Alexander stopped halfway through the gate. "I can hotwire cars," he snapped. "How do you think I got here?"

Honey shrugged. His glare softened. He opened his mouth, and Honey thought—hoped?—he'd say something else. A proper goodbye. Even *see you later* would do.

But he just gave a nod, short and curt, averting his eyes before the movement was finished. He vanished out of the gate, footsteps fading as he ran into the night.

"Crap," Honey said softly. "Think I got attached to the little freak."

Sadie huffed a pained laugh into her hair. Her hands were a horror show of burns and there was a new hole in her shoulder, not to mention the chest wound that hadn't yet closed up. Honey foresaw a lot of animal blood and bathtubs in their future.

Honey waved up at Rosaline. "Sorry for breaking your fence."

"Eh." Rosaline examined the hole in her fence, black

blood seeping into her lawn, the headless body in front of her geranium bushes. "I was gonna tear it down anyway. That thing was getting old. Do you two want to come in? I have pig's blood in the fridge."

Sadie sent Honey a wary look. *Can we trust her?*

"We'd love to," said Honey. She let Sadie ease her to her feet, leaning on her as spots danced in front of her eyes.

Rosaline swung the front door open, flicking on the light to reveal a cozy front hall painted pale purple. She toed her fuzzy slippers off and gestured down for the girls to do the same.

"Hey," Honey said as she sat down to peel her boots off. It didn't seem safe to bend down with her head still spinning. "Did you know your house looks just like the *Gilmore Girls* house?"

"The *Gilmore Girls* house looks like *my* house," Rosaline corrected, heading down the hall and into a room that smelled like spices. "I had it first!"

"She's cool," Honey whispered to Sadie.

A faint laugh drifted out from the room Rosaline had vanished into.

Sadie nodded distractedly. She was staring around at the hall, its vibrant colors, and photographs hung on the walls. Group photos, mostly. Barbecues and beaches, people and light and laughter.

Honey bumped Sadie's uninjured shoulder. "Not very shitty and small."

Sadie blinked. "No," she said, voice small and impossibly tired and more hopeful than Honey had heard it in a long time.

Rosaline sat them down in the kitchen. She poured a mug of hot cocoa then the microwave pinged and she lifted out two more steaming mugs. Her charm bracelet clinked against the chipped porcelain as she placed all three on the worn table, keeping one for herself.

Honey leaned over the mugs. "Which one's mine?"

Sadie gave her a look and took the mug filled with warm pig's blood. Rosaline had put two mugs in the microwave while she was fixing Honey hot cocoa on the stove. Sadie took a sip and her entire face creased up.

"Oh god," she rasped. "That's—"

"Revolting," Rosaline agreed, sipping blood from her own mug with a grimace. "Two days old, keep it in the fridge so it doesn't spoil. Works in a pinch."

Sadie nodded, taking another cringing sip. A black piece of skin flecked off her knuckles.

"Big baby," Honey told her. She rubbed Sadie's back, eyeing the mug of hot cocoa in front of her.

Sadie followed her gaze, frowning.

Honey thought about telling her she didn't want to cry in front of a stranger. Then she took the mug and pressed it to her mouth, inhaling the sweet scent—duller than it would've been half an hour ago, but infinitely more appetizing—before letting it stream into her mouth.

It was...good. Not *human blood straight from the tap* good, nothing would ever taste *that* good again, but it was good. Comforting. Like her mom used to make, if it had a few more sugars dropped in.

Honey blinked back tears, clearing her throat. "Human blood makes her heal faster. Like, a *lot*."

"'Course," Rosaline said. Her voice was calm and understanding, but her eyes were sharp as they flicked over Sadie. "Newborn?"

Sadie nodded.

"Struggling more than others your age?"

Sadie glanced at Honey and nodded again.

"Hmm." Rosaline pulled her dressing gown cord tighter around her waist, pudgy arms settling over the string. She had that same pale sheen all vampires had, but it wasn't sallow. Her brown hair shone, plaited in an elaborate rope down her back. She looked maybe forty-five years old, which could mean anything.

"How old *are* you?" Honey asked.

Rosaline smiled. She had a nice smile, wide and stretchy. "I am eight hundred years young."

Honey didn't know what else to say to that other than, "You look great."

"Thank you."

Sadie forced down another mouthful of pig's blood. "Is that old? For a vampire?"

"Oh, yes. The average age for a vampire is two hundred and fifty." Rosaline's grin grew at their expressions. "They can't adapt," she explained. Her smile dimmed as she reached over to toy with her charm bracelet. It was heavy with charms, all of them different sizes and metals, all bronze. Honey spotted a knife, a bowler hat, a book, a fish. Some of them pristine and sharp, others clumsy and dull with age.

Sadie asked, "What do you eat?"

"Animals. *Live* ones," Rosaline added when they both looked dubiously at the pig's blood. "And we have a blood donor, a friend of the family, who comes over a few times a month."

"Cool," Honey said faintly, trying to think of what came next in this weird conversation. "So...what do you do?"

"For the last decade? I'm a teacher. But I've done all sorts." Rosaline leaned back in her chair, clasping her mug to her chest. She didn't sleep, so the dressing gown had to be for maximum coziness. Not a bad life.

"Now, the question burning the back of *my* mind," Rosaline said, "is what the heck led you here with a baby vampire hunter and a dead sire?"

Honey looked at Sadie. Sadie looked at Honey.

"I'm shot," Sadie said. "*And* burned."

"I just turned human," Honey argued. "I'm exhausted."

"*You're* the storyteller."

Honey sighed. "Okay, so. Last year I go to this party and I get in the band's van, like an idiot. They drink my blood and dump my body at the side of the road. But surprise, I'm not dead! Not properly, anyway. So I rope

Sadie into a road trip to kill my sire, and after some trial and error, we totally do it. Except the one who I thought was my sire wasn't actually my sire, *my* sire got away. Then Sadie gets hurt, like, *mortally* wounded, and I turn her to save her life. We don't know where the hell my sire's gone, so we go home. We're *this* close to graduating high school and jetting off to Cali. Our true crime YouTuber friend messages us about our sire in North Carolina, but before we set off on murder road trip part two, this annoying little asshole hunter attacks us and says he'll kill us if the sire stuff doesn't work."

Rosaline's gaze slid back to Sadie, who was taking the rest of the pig's blood like a shot of medicine she had to choke down.

"We told him he was her sire too," Honey explained. "So he comes with us. We drag the trip out, try to make him like Sadie so he won't kill her after I get human'd and Sadie stays fangy. Which *totally* worked, because I'm a genius. And...now we're here."

Sadie lowered her empty mug with a shudder. Honey took her wrist right above the burned skin, and Sadie looked over with that same look of surprise she'd had when Honey put her arm around her in the diner. Like she'd forgotten they weren't in their tiny hometown, pretending not to know each other in the school halls.

Rosaline nodded slowly. "And where to from here?"

Sadie looked away. Honey's heart clenched.

"Um," Honey said, and laughed. "I was planning on Berkeley? But if Sadie's still, um, struggling—"

"She's going to college," Sadie said sharply.

Rosaline hummed. "And you, vampling?"

Sadie gave her a suspicious look, like she couldn't tell if the nickname was making fun of her or not. "I'm..."

She trailed off. Her hand was stiff under Honey's.

"That boy said you can't go home," Rosaline said, voice soft. Not *too* soft, not the kind that would make Sadie think she was being pitied and tense up even more. This was quiet, understanding. Like she'd been in the same position, once.

"I'll figure it out," Sadie said roughly. Blackness welled up in the corner of one eye. She pulled her hand free of Honey to wipe at it.

Rosaline hummed again. "Or you could stay here."

Sadie stared at her. Honey did, too, but then she was too busy surreptitiously glancing around to see any signs of secret passages to the basement, or cult stuff, or a murder wall. She was too *nice*. Milly had been nice, but she didn't offer up her *home*.

"As of last year, my latest foster children have all moved out," Rosaline said. "You could say my nest is empty."

Honey thought back to the rows of photographs in the front hall. Graduations and dinners and weddings, the same faces in so many frames.

"You'd just...let me live with you," Sadie said.

"And help you with your hunger. Once it was my specialty, helping newborns. People sent them to me.

Other times they sought me out. It's been a while since I had a proper problem case. Should be fun."

"*Problem case,*" Honey repeated mockingly. "That's so—"

Her stomach rumbled. It wasn't *that* loud, but to vampires it probably sounded like a train thundering past.

"Right." Rosaline stood, adjusting her dressing gown. "New human. I should've put something on for you right away. What would you like?"

Honey didn't have to think about it. "Do you have hash browns?"

"I'll put the air fryer on," Rosaline said, politely ignoring how Honey welled up over it. She went over to the freezer and crouched down, pulling it open to reveal a surprising amount of goods, including a brand-name box of hash browns Honey hadn't seen in a year.

"While those are cooking," she announced, "I'll go clean up the body in the yard."

chapter
fourteen

THE KITCHEN SMELLED like the rosemary and oil Rosaline had spritzed on the hash browns before sliding them in. It was an improvement over pig's blood, which Sadie still smelled if she bent her head too close to her mug.

"So," Honey said as the air fryer whirred. "North Carolina isn't...*that* far away from California."

Sadie stared at her. "It's literally on the opposite side of the country. It's *forty hours* of driving."

"People do long distance," Honey insisted. "People do long distance for *years.*"

"You think long distance is stupid."

"I think *you're* stupid." Honey curled a hand around Sadie's wrist again, her fingers warm and soft above the numbness creeping over Sadie's burned hands. "Us not being together is stupider."

She bumped her nose into Sadie's cheek. Her breath smelled cocoa-sweet, her hair musty with grass and stiff with black goo. And under it all, the siren call of blood. Honey's pulse fluttered in her neck, so close and so tempting.

Sadie leaned back, digging her nails into the underside of the table. Rosaline would've seen worse, if she made a habit of taking in newborn vampires.

Honey groaned. "I can see you freaking out. *Quit* it. We have so much life left to live—"

"And I want you to live it!"

"I will! I'll go to college, I'll make friends who are into the same cool, weird shit I'm into, we'll call."

"For how long? If there's no cure, I don't know when I'm going to be...functional."

"You're *going* to find a way to live with this. And live *well*." Honey squeezed her wrist, right above where the burn started. "Even if you stay a vampire."

Sadie tried to turn away. Honey caught her chin, twisting her back to meet Honey's gaze. Her flimsy human fingers pressed into the hard lines of her jaw. Sadie imagined breaking free. Imagined running off into the night. Imagined lunging forward and sinking her fangs into Honey's neck, ripping until blood flowed into the shirt they'd bought at a thrift shop two towns over.

She wanted it. The blood, the carnage, drinking until she was finally, blissfully full. But she wanted it the same way she sometimes wanted to throw her phone off tall places, or chew her nails until they bled.

There was another want underneath it. Quieter, less dramatic. No euphoria, just...calm. She wanted to sit there with her face in Honey's familiar hands, heat leaching through her fingers and into Sadie's skin, sinking down all the way to her heart.

Sadie closed her eyes.

The air fryer dinged.

"Oh my *god*," Honey said, voice so thick with relieved tears Sadie didn't even mind it when her hands slipped away.

The yard was clean. Mostly.

The broken fenceposts were gone, as was the body. But there were still woodchips and smaller pieces scattering the bushes, black blood staining the grass.

"I'll mow it tomorrow," Rosaline told them as they stood on the porch. "Anyone asks, I'll say we had a tie-dye incident."

Sadie nodded at the fence. "And that?"

"Teaching teenagers to drive," Rosaline said dryly. She started down the porch steps, then paused. "Sure you don't want me to bring you something? Uber Eats, but with woodland animals."

She looked pleased at her own reference. Sadie wondered how hard it would be, keeping up with centuries of technological advancement. Eight hundred *years*. What was even *happening* eight hundred years ago?

Sadie tried to remember what period of history the thirteenth century was and came up blank. She'd ask Honey later. Honey had all sorts of knowledge that was utterly useless until it wasn't. She'd kill it at college trivia nights.

"No," Sadie answered. "I'll come."

Honey cleared her throat and struck a casual pose against the columns holding up the porch. "You don't want to...?"

She tilted her head. Her hair fell away, exposing the long line of her throat.

Sadie swallowed. "I don't want Rosaline to have to beat me back with a shovel."

"Hot," Honey said. She shook her strawberry blonde hair back into place. "Happy hunting. I'm gonna make more hash browns."

Sadie kissed her cheek. It tasted like salt. Honey had cried the whole way through her first helping.

She pulled back, ignoring the part of her that wanted to dive back in and bite through Honey's salty cheek.

"Happy hash-browning," she said, and followed Rosaline into the woods.

Rosaline stuck to her side the whole time. Feet bare, dressing gown streaming in the wind. By the end of it, the gown was smeared with animal blood and dirt and feathers.

"Started breeding free-range chickens a few years back," Rosaline said, unbothered by her ruined clothing. "They're doing surprisingly well."

Sadie nodded, picking a splinter of bone from her

teeth. After the chickens, they'd lucked out and found a herd of deer munching grass in a clearing. When Sadie came out of her blood frenzy, the clearing was splattered with blood, her clothes drenched with it. Rosaline had been on the other side of the clearing, healing a baby deer's leg and sending it scampering after its escaped family.

"We need to work on your venom," was all she'd said when she noticed Sadie watching.

Her face was still smeared crimson, and she didn't bother to wipe the mess away as she walked next to Sadie.

Sadie always wiped her face straight after. She couldn't imagine not wanting to, even if just to lick her fingers clean.

She sucked blood off her lower lip. "Is there a way to change back?"

"Without killing your sire? Not that I know of." Rosaline gave her a knowing look, like she knew exactly what Sadie thought about *that* option. "But I can help you look."

Sadie shook her head, infuriating tears welling in her eyes. "You're eight hundred years old. If *you* haven't found anything—"

"*There are more things in heaven and earth than are dreamt of in your philosophy,*" Rosaline said. It sounded like Shakespeare. Sadie didn't know which one. She'd barely scraped through English.

"Sure," Sadie croaked. "Great. That fixes things."

A black tear spilled down her cheek. She scrubbed at it, smearing blood and feathers.

Rosaline stopped and stretched. She seemed so at ease Sadie almost hated her.

"It gets better," Rosaline said as she lowered her arms. "You won't feel like this forever."

"What if it doesn't?"

"It will. It doesn't *go away*. It just gets *less*."

Sadie snorted, wiping her messy cheeks.

Rosaline didn't speak again until they reached the house. As they climbed up the back porch, Rosaline paused.

"It can be a good life," she told Sadie, holding open the back door. "Really."

Sadie sniffed. The back door led into the kitchen. Inside, the leftover scent of oil and herbs rushed to meet her. Colorful walls, windowsills crammed with nick-nacks, homemade mugs hanging next to the cabinets.

Sadie wanted to believe she could have a good life. She wanted it so badly.

Rosaline nodded down at Sadie's hands. "Healing yet?"

Sadie held them up. Shades of pale pink showed through the numb black crusts of her fingers.

"Slowly," she said.

Honey was waiting for her in the spare room. At first

Sadie thought she was asleep, eyes closed and breathing slow as she sat back against the bedframe.

Then Sadie eased the door shut and Honey's eyes struggled open as she lurched up from the pillow she'd stacked behind her.

"'M still awake," she mumbled. She blinked hard, roving her gaze over Sadie's scrubbed cheeks and damp hair, her newly bandaged shoulder. She grimaced at Sadie's burned fingers.

"Palms got the worst of it," Sadie said, jumping up onto the bed next to her. "That's what I get for holding onto that ax for so long. But my chest is almost healed."

She pulled her shirt down. The hole underneath her collarbones had turned into a shriveled white divot, barely big enough to fit a pinkie into.

Honey dropped her head onto her shoulder. Her eyelids drooped.

Sadie pushed her hair back. "How's your first night being human again?"

Honey grunted. "It's morning. Like...three a.m."

"Night-night, spidermonkey."

Honey reached out groggily, grabbing Sadie's arm. "Not yet!"

"What do you want?"

"Lullaby." Honey leaned over the side of the bed, cursing quietly until she resurfaced with Sadie's guitar. She pushed it into Sadie's hands and then slid down to lie against the pillows, waiting.

Sadie curled her marred fingers over the strings. "I'm still kinda numb," she warned.

Honey made a fart noise. "You *just* said your palms got most of the heat. Power through it, wimp."

"*Wimp*," Sadie whispered, mock-offended. She pressed hard, the strings biting into her skin. Her fingertips tingled. She plucked carefully, building confidence until she could fall into that same song they'd played on stage, the same tune they had in every song they invented.

She sung softly. "*Worst week of my life, best time I ever had...*"

"*Watch the teeth, baby,*" Honey whispered. Her eyes drifted shut. Her face slackened.

For the first time in over a year, Honey Williams slept.

chapter
fifteen

HONEY SAT ALONE on the swings, looking out over the empty playground. In one more week she would be at college and the park would be demolished to make way for a baseball field.

She pushed herself back and forth, listening to the rubber creak underneath her. Wind through the trees. A fly buzzing.

She closed her eyes.

"Hi Honey," came a voice right next to her ear. "I'm home."

Honey grinned. She opened her eyes to see Sadie in the swing next to her. Baggy jeans, flannel shirt, battered Converse sneakers, leaning sideways to bump Honey's shoulder.

Honey bumped back. "I still think it's stupid we walked here separately. People can still walk by and see us sitting together."

"Oh yeah. *So* many people." Sadie looked out over

the empty park, its broken slide and rotting seesaw. "Look at this place, they're practically falling over each other."

Honey laughed. It had been a long, hot summer. She'd signed yearbooks and posed for graduation photos and even hugged Britney and Summer before they left town. They'd hugged back, surprised and pleased, everybody making hangout promises they all knew would never be kept.

Honey didn't hang out with anyone that summer. She ate comfort food and made Facebook friends with her future dorm-mate. She took long, luxurious naps on a ratty beach towel in her backyard, her skin going from vampire-pale to its usual golden tan.

Honey asked, "Did you see your dad?"

Sadie nodded.

"How'd it go?"

"Pretty good. Took a while to make him believe me. I had to fly around and cut my arm open." Sadie pulled up her sleeve to show Honey the deep gouge beneath the elbow, still oozing black.

Honey made a face. "Ew. But he's on board now?"

"Uh-huh. Sending me money and everything. He got very weird about Rosaline not charging me rent." Sadie smoothed her sleeve back down, ignoring the dark stain. Then she stopped and cocked her head, listening hard.

Honey froze. "What? What is it?"

"Squirrel. Sorry." Sadie smiled sheepishly.

Honey shoved her. Sadie rocked sideways, like one

little push had any impact. Like she couldn't stay perfectly still if Honey slammed into her at a full sprint.

Sadie asked, "Have they tried anything?"

Honey shook her head. Alexander's parents had only talked to Honey once, after bumping into her at the supermarket. Honey had been looking for fresh cilantro —it had always tasted like soap to her and she wanted to see if getting vampired and then un-vampired had changed her tastebuds—when she felt something cool against the back of her neck.

She'd turned around to find a middle-aged couple looming behind her with stiff, polite smiles. They were blonde and tidy and looked like the kind of people who would leave stern messages for neighbors who decorated too much for Halloween.

"My car keys got away from me," the woman said, a flash of silver vanishing up her sleeve. "Sorry about that."

Maybe it was car keys. But Honey knew in her heart it had been a knife with a diamond on the wooden hilt. Seeing if she burned.

"Hey," the man said, his blue eyes unnervingly focused on her. "Aren't you the girl who did performance art with our Alexander?"

"Yes," Honey said after she'd suppressed a shiver at the man's unrelenting gaze. "Right. Fun guy."

They both blinked. It was probably the first time anyone had described their son as 'fun.'

"I heard it was a hoot," Mrs. White said. "Wish we could've been there."

Honey laughed nervously. It was strangely easy to picture this cardigan-clad couple wielding silver crossbows. Something about their smiles, the pure *threat* hiding behind that cookie-cutter facade.

"We've been having trouble getting in touch," Mr. White told her. "Bad cell providers, you know how it is. Have you heard from him?"

They stood there in the vegetable aisle, staring each other down. A shiver ran up Honey's back. How much had Alexander told them?

"No," Honey said truthfully. "I haven't heard anything. He moved out of state, right? To live with his cousins?"

"Right," they said in unison.

Honey twirled a strand of strawberry blonde hair around her finger. "Kinda weird time to do that, right? A few months before the end of sophomore year?"

Tense seconds passed. Mrs. White let out a shrill laugh.

"Well," she said brightly. "You know Alexander."

Honey's stomach twisted, imagining growing up with these people. A thousand unanswered questions ran through her head in that moment—would they really *chase him down*, what would it entail, why did he look so sad when she asked him about siblings—but she shoved them down. Even if she had asked, they wouldn't tell.

"Not much," she'd said, giving them a sunny smile. "Well! See ya. Wouldn't wanna be ya."

With that, she'd walked off, her spine tingling,

expecting a yell or an arrow to follow her at any second. But nothing had come.

"Alexander was right," Honey told Sadie. "Once they made sure I was human, they left me alone."

Sadie hummed. It wasn't a relieved hum. It was a hum that implied Honey's observational skills were a lot worse since she lost her vampire powers.

Honey flicked Sadie's bangs. "But they'll totally shoot you if they see you."

"Good thing I'm getting out of here in a few minutes." Sadie grinned.

Honey grinned back, so delighted at getting to see Sadie smile that the smile was only a little marred by their inevitable parting. She reached between their swings and took Sadie's cold hand.

"So how's Fester? Bloodlust manageable yet?"

"Yeah, I'm totally cured," Sadie said flatly. She looked away. "It's...getting better? Rosaline still has to smack me with a baseball bat whenever I feed from the blood guy, but I'm improving with the venom."

"Training wheels," Honey said, squeezing Sadie's cool fingers. "Cut it out with that sad dog look. The hunger gets *less*. Then you'll follow me to Cali. Probably before I finish undergrad."

"Yeah, and then postgrad. Then another postgrad. Then you'll find all these messed up new bugs—"

"*Beautiful* new bugs," Honey corrected.

"And you'll be my hot MILF. And then my grand-

MILF." Sadie's mouth twisted as she traced heart in the playground bark with her shoe.

Honey tried another grin. "Is this your way of saying you won't like me when my boobs sag?"

"I will abandon you immediately," Sadie said, voice squeaky with tears and adoration.

Honey took her chin in her hands. Sadie tried to resist, but only for a moment. She let Honey twist her face back to meet her expectant gaze.

"We'll see what happens," Honey said gently. "Just like anyone else."

Sadie nodded tightly. She sniffed, wiping a black speck from the corner of her eye. "I really should get going."

She started to stand. Honey yanked her back down. Sadie yielded, just like she'd rocked with Honey's shove and let Honey pull her back to face her. All that strength and she still let Honey pull her around, just like when they were kids on this same playground.

"I have to..." Sadie trailed off as Honey pulled her hair over her shoulder, exposing the long line of her neck.

Honey tilted her head. "Go on."

Sadie swallowed, her face filling with reluctant desire. "You did hear the bit about Rosaline smacking me with a baseball bat, right?"

"Wimp," Honey told her. She craned her neck further, watching Sadie's pupils expand. "Do it. I trust you."

She also had a silver knife tucked in her skirt, but Sadie didn't need to know that.

Sadie hesitated. "You sure?"

"Dead sure." Honey grinned, her voice only shaking slightly. "Remember to venom me up."

Sadie nodded. She ghosted her cool lips over Honey's neck. She pressed an icy kiss to the hollow of Honey's throat. Then she sunk her teeth in.

Honey hissed. For a moment it was just pain, sharp and shocking. She bit her tongue, fumbling for the knife hidden in her skirt. Before she could reach it, a flicker of euphoria bled into her neck.

Honey heard herself gasp, strangled. The venom hit her nervous system and bloomed, climbing up her veins until all of her sang.

"'S nice," Honey rasped.

Sadie hummed, strained, into her neck. She pulled back, shaking with effort, eyes squeezed shut.

The euphoria faded, leaving Honey shaking.

"Whoa," she said, and giggled. "Head rush."

Sadie nodded tightly. She opened her eyes, black seeping away to reveal those green eyes Honey loved so much. She reached a trembling hand to touch Honey's bite wound. The ragged skin tingled as the wound started to close.

Honey caught Sadie's hand. "Don't. I want the mark."

The tingle in her neck stopped. Pain rushed to replace it, making Honey wince.

Sadie's hand hovered over the torn skin. "Are you sure?"

"Dead sure," Honey repeated. "I'll be this super sexy girl at freshman orientation with a mysterious new scar. *Everybody* will want to talk to me."

Sadie wiped her wet lips. She was still shaking, pulling her gaze away from Honey's bleeding neck.

Honey kissed her. Sadie's mouth was cold but the blood was so warm as Honey smeared it between their mouths. Honey's head swam—from blood loss or from Sadie, she didn't know.

She kept her eyes closed as she drew back, their foreheads still touching.

"Have fun at college," Sadie whispered. She linked their pinkies together and squeezed. Honey squeezed back, and then the hand was gone and so was the cool skin on her forehead.

Honey opened her eyes. The playground was empty. She giggled to herself, reaching up to touch the stinging holes in her neck.

"Till death, bitch," she screamed into the afternoon air.

A laugh drifted out of the trees. A triumphant shout followed it, there and gone. Sadie was already so far away that Honey barely heard it, but that was okay. She didn't need to hear.

She knew what it said.

END.

thank you

Thank you so much for reading Honeycraves!

If you want to support me, please leave a review on Goodreads, Amazon or any social media of your choice.

Sign up to my newsletter for exciting updates and the first book in my spooky sapphic YA romance series, BABYLOVE! Head on over to isbelleauthor.com to get your free ebook.

acknowledgments

First off, thank you to the awesome readers who read this series! It was so much fun writing these girls, thanks for coming along for the ride.

Thank you to my cover artist Sophie Zuckerman (@dextrose.png on Insta!) for another baller cover.

Thank you to my wonderful formatter, Edward Giordano, and Catriona Turner, my editor. You're consistently amazing, and I'd be lost without you.

about the author

I. S. Belle writes LGBT Romance, Paranormal and Horror Young Adult books. She works in a bookstore in New Zealand and stops to pat dogs in the street. If you have a dog and your local bookshop allows pets - for the love of booksellers, please bring them in.

She has a Creative Writing Masters from the International Institute of Modern Letters. You can find her on Tiktok @i.s.belle_writes or on Instagram @isbelleauthor.

also by

I. S. Belle

LGBT+ Young Adult Fiction

BABYLOVE SERIES

BABYLOVE

SUGARSNAP

SWEETHEARTS

ZOMBABE

ZOMBABE

HONEYBLOODS SERIES

HONEYBLOODS

HONEYBITES

HONEYCRAVES

GIRLS NIGHT

GIRLS NIGHT

also by

Isabelle Taylor

Cozy Monster Adult Romance Fiction

CLAW HAVEN

SNOWED IN WITH A SUCCUBUS

ACCIDENTALLY WEDDED TO A WEREWOLF

(COMING LATE 2024)

Milton Keynes UK
Ingram Content Group UK Ltd.
UKHW031049300724
1073UKWH00003B/122